MY HERO ACADEMIA

SCHOOL BRIEFS

2

Training Camp: The Inside Story

ORIGINAL CONCEPT BY
KOHEI HORIKOSHI

WRITTEN BY
ANRI YOSHI

U.A. HIGH SCHOOL

Hero Course: Class 1-A

zuku Midoriya

Birthday: July 15
Quirk: One For All

Katsuki Bakugo

Birthday: April 20
Quirk: Explosion

Shoto Todoroki

Birthday: January 11
Quirk:
Half-Cold Half-Hot

Tenya Ida

Birthday: August 22
Quirk: Engine

Fumikage Tokoyami

Birthday: October 30
Quirk: Dark Shadow

Minoru Mineta

Birthday: October 8
Quirk: Pop Off

Ochaco Uraraka

Birthday:
December 27
Quirk: Zero Gravity

Momo Yaoyorozu

Birthday:
September 23
Quirk: Creation

Tsuyu Asui

Birthday: February 12
Quirk: Frog

Yuga Aoyama

Birthday: May 30
Quirk: Navel Laser

Mina Ashido

Birthday: July 30
Quirk: Acid

Mashirao Ojiro

Birthday: May 28
Quirk: Tail

Denki Kaminari

Birthday: June 29
Quirk: Electrification

Eijiro Kirishima

Birthday: October 16
Quirk: Hardening

Koji Koda

Birthday: February 1
Quirk: Anivoice

Rikido Sato

Birthday: June 19
Quirk: Sugar Rush

STUDENT ROLL CALL

Mezo Shoji

Birthday: February 15
Quirk: Dupli-Arms

Kyoka Jiro

Birthday: August 1
Quirk: Earphone Jack

Hanta Sero

Birthday: July 28
Quirk: Tape

Toru Hagakure

Birthday: June 16
Quirk: Invisibility

Hero Course: Class 1-B

Itsuka Kendo

Birthday:
September 9
Quirk: Big Fist

Ibara Shiozaki

Birthday:
September 8
Quirk: Vines

Reiko Yanagi

Birthday: February 11
Quirk: Poltergeist

Yui Kodai

Birthday:
December 19
Quirk: Size

Neito Monoma

Birthday: May 13
Quirk: Copy

Tetsutetsu Tetsutetsu

Birthday: October 16
Quirk: Steel

Juzo Honenuki

Birthday: June 20
Quirk: Softening

Nirengeki Shoda

Birthday: February 2
Quirk: Twin Impact

STORY

People in this world possess exceptional abilities called "Quirks." Some use their Quirks in pursuit of peace, while others choose to commit crimes with their powers, but they're all part of the same superpowered society. Izuku Midoriya may have been born Quirkless, but he nonetheless gets into U.A. High School, an academy for heroes in training. There, he walks the path toward becoming a true hero! The stories in this book offer a heretofore unrevealed glimpse at the everyday lives of the students attending U.A. High.

MY HERO ACADEMIA

SCHOOL BRIEFS

CONTENTS

2

Training Camp: The Inside Story

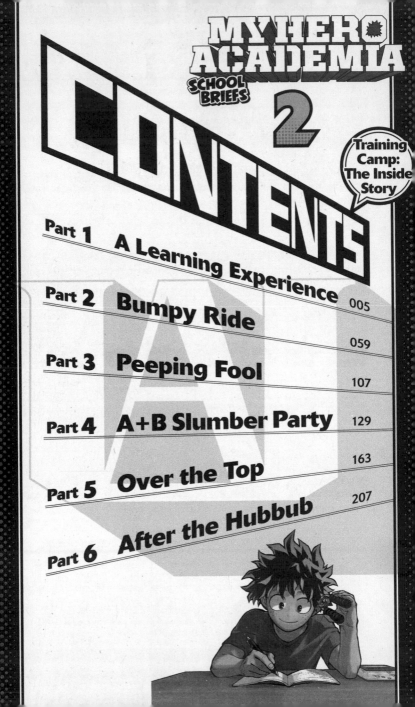

Part 1
A Learning Experience

*BOOK: CLASSICAL LITERATURE

It was the final Sunday of June, with skies as clear as could be. The perfect sort of day to go out and about, before the weighty descent of summer heat. But Izuku Midoriya was hunched over his desk at home, indifferent to the gorgeous weather just outside his window. After all, even the students of U.A. High's legendary Hero Course were still, first and foremost, students, with all the usual tests to study for. While Midoriya's right hand solved math problems, his left clenched an exercise gripper—the only thing hinting at his hero-in-training status.

He'd been in a rough place one year ago.

In order to receive a Quirk from his personal hero, All Might, Midoriya had hauled an entire beach park's worth of trash to turn his limp-noodle body into a suitably muscled vessel. At the same time, he'd studied tirelessly for U.A.'s entrance exam, so he'd had to teach his hands to multitask on the fly. Now, he could almost look back with fond memories on the time he'd collapsed from fatigue, because saving people would eventually demand that sort of strength.

"Phew."

Satisfied with his progress for the moment, Midoriya put down his pencil and gripper, raised his eyes, and stared at the poster of All Might on his wall, which portrayed the hero with his trademark voluminous muscles and gleaming white teeth.

Respect. Reassurance. Rapture.

All Might was an endless source of inspiration for Midoriya that allowed him to tap into a geyser of energy within himself. All to become as great a hero as his idol.

"All right, back to it!" he said, turning the page of the textbook. Midoriya's grades in ordinary subject areas were among the best in his class, so he wasn't particularly stressed. Still, failure was not an option, since participation in the upcoming training camp was contingent on passing these final exams.

"Hope Kaminari and them can pull this off..."

Midoriya's less gifted classmates had freaked out when they learned the penalty for failure, so he spared a thought for them. Then again, hadn't Momo Yaoyorozu offered to tutor them? If anyone could help the stragglers, it would be the biggest brain in the class. Midoriya imagined the prim and proper Yaoyorozu in tutor mode as he got back to his own studying. Hopefully, all twenty members of class 1-A would get to make the trip.

UA

Just as Midoriya sent out his good vibes, Denki Kaminari, Kyoka Jiro, and the other students in question arrived at Yaoyorozu's house.

"Eh? Is this the place...?" asked Kaminari.

"No way... Looks like an embassy or something," muttered a shocked Hanta Sero.

Beside them, Mashirao Ojiro double-checked the map on his phone.

"Nope, this is the right address."

"Omigod, megamansion!" shouted Mina Ashido, with all of her usual candidness.

A massive, stately front gate towered before the kids, with a wall just as high extending in either direction, seemingly without end. They had met up at the nearest train station and, on the walk to Yaoyorozu's place, had noticed the wall and wondered what sort of property it defended. Slowly the truth had dawned on them, prompting excitement from Kaminari and Ashido and creeping dread from the other three. If this really were a foreign embassy, and if they'd been spies planning to steal state secrets, the gate and wall alone would've made them think twice about the mission.

Everyone knew Yaoyorozu was rich, but this rich? It was enough to trigger a fight-or-flight response. Jiro barely had time to furrow her brow, though, before the gate started to open with a smoothness that belied its size and spoke to its craftsmanship.

"Miss Jiro, Miss Ashido, Mr. Kaminari, Mr. Sero, and Mr. Ojiro, I presume?"

Beyond the gate was a petite man with gentle features, in formal wear. Though his salt-and-pepper hair suggested he was seventy-something, he stood with

the ramrod straightness of a much-younger man.

The five kids weren't quite sure how to respond to such deference from an older gentleman. Sensing this, he gave them a dignified smile that sent a web of wrinkles racing across his face.

"Welcome, one and all. I am Uchimura, the Yaoyorozu household's butler. Miss Momo is expecting you, so by all means, do come in."

"S-sure," said Jiro.

They awkwardly followed Uchimura.

"A real-life butler! They do exist!" gasped Ashido as quietly as her excitement would allow.

"If they've got a butler, you think they've got maids, too?" asked Kaminari in hushed tones.

"Guys! Just stop…" scolded Jiro.

"Yes, the household employs maids as well," beamed Uchimura, not at all put off by their lack of decorum. A butler managing such a prestigious property couldn't very well sweat the small stuff, after all.

Jiro and friends passed through a beautifully manicured garden the size of a small forest until at last the house came into view. House? No. Not even "mansion" would do this justice. This was practically a castle, as majestic as those found in old Europe, and the kids were tempted to run back to the front gate and scan the neighborhood for evidence that they were still in Japan.

"Welcome," said a group of maids in unison from within the open doors of the front hall. The visitors gaped, too stunned to speak, as a woman rushed toward them from deeper within the house.

"Hello there! I'm Mrs. Yaoyorozu. How wonderful to meet my Momo's dear friends..."

Jiro managed a "H-hello, ma'am."

The smiling mother was the spitting image of their friend, aged up and somehow a bit warmer.

"And five of you! I'm so very glad that Momo has already made so many fr— Oh. You there..."

"Huh?" said Jiro.

The girl instinctively glanced at her own clothes, since that was where Mrs. Yaoyorozu's gaze now fell. The customized collar on Jiro's T-shirt was ripped open wide enough to expose her shoulders, and to this she had added leather pants and a studded leather cuff around one wrist. It was a tame outfit by her standards.

Something wrong with my look?

Jiro thought she noticed Mrs. Yaoyorozu's gently curved eyebrows scrunch together for a second, though her smile quickly returned.

"Ahem, Momo is making preparations in the auditorium. Let's get you over there."

"Shall I...?" began Uchimura.

"No, allow me," answered Mrs. Yaoyorozu, motioning the kids toward the inner corridors. They followed at a relaxed pace, glancing about all the while at floral wallpaper, marble floors, ornate vases, and paintings famous enough to recognize.

"Like the Palace of Versailles... Not that I've ever been."

"Right...? Bet this's what it's like, though."

"Totally..."

Jiro was just as stunned, even if she wasn't as vocal about it as her friends. Ashido, on the other hand...

"You're telling me Momoyao lives here? She really is a princess, then!"

"Momoyao?" asked Mrs. Yaoyorozu, turning to her guests.

"Um, Momoyao is just what we call Momoyao... I mean, what we call Momo. Your daughter, that is," stammered Jiro.

"A nickname, then! Momoyao... Like some lovely, exotic plant. What nickname would you give me, then?"

"Well, since you're Momoyao's mom, how about Mamayao!" Ashido blurted out without missing a beat.

"Wonderful. By all means, call me Mamayao."

"Sure thing, Mamayao!"

"Yes, ma'am. I mean, Mamayao," said Jiro.

Mamayao's smile suggested that she genuinely loved Ashido's off-the-cuff suggestion, but the earlier, stern look still weighed on Jiro's mind. Did her friend's mother have something against her outfit? The others were just as underdressed, though...

"Something fascinating about the floor?" asked Kaminari.

Jiro looked up. The boy couldn't pass a test to save his life, but he was sharp in other ways.

"Shut up, you. And yes, I just happen to be taking in the sights."

"Real nice place, yeah? And I bet it stays cool in the summer. Wish we could stay over."

"I don't."

"What's up with you, huh?"

Jiro couldn't help but sigh at Kaminari's happy-go-lucky face. No point in angsting about her fashion choices now. Not when they'd come here to study.

"You're the one who needs to focus, Mister Bottom-of-the-Class," spat Jiro.

"So everyone keeps reminding me. That's why I'm placing my fate in Professor Yaoyorozu's capable hands."

"Momoyao won't always be there to save you."

"I know, I know. Gimme a break."

They soon arrived at the "auditorium," which was no understatement. In one corner of the grand space was a long table furnished with chairs.

"Momo, your friends are here," announced Mamayao.

"So sorry I couldn't greet you all myself... I was busy fretting about what materials to prepare," said Momo Yaoyorozu.

A pair of glasses lent their friend a scholarly look, while the flush of her cheeks and the glint in her eyes told them just how eager she was about their study party.

"I'll leave you children to it, then... But I'll send some tea over later. Be a good teacher now, Momo."

"Yes, Mother."

Jiro gave a small, secret sigh of relief as Mamayao exited the room and shut the door. She felt guilty about this in light of Yaoyorozu's clear enthusiasm, but luckily the latter was too worked up to notice.

"Without delay, let us begin the tutoring!"

"Woo-hoo!" shouted Ashido, while Ojiro responded with a more subdued "Please and thanks."

"Take it away, Professorozu!" said Sero.

"Screw this up and I won't get to go to training camp, Teach!" added Kaminari.

"I said not to put that on her, you," chided Jiro.

"Not to worry, friends! You can count on me to raise your test scores!" shot back an exuberant Yaoyorozu. She thrived on being needed like this, and their expectations only served to light a fire under her.

U.A.

At a nearby library, another study group was about to hit the books.

"C'monnn, Bakugo!"

"Cram it, broomhead!"

Eijiro Kirishima and Katsuki Bakugo sat at a sunlit table by a window and were already earning stares from other library patrons. Stares that implied "Shhh."

"Sorry, folks!"

Kirishima's panicked apology was just as loud, prompting an older man to say "Spirited youngsters, aren't you?" through a strained smile. It was Sunday, so the library was packed with families, students doing research, and the elderly.

It had actually been Yaoyorozu who had led the two boys to this spot, in a way. While she had the best grades in the class, Bakugo was ranked third, so when Yaoyorozu had agreed to tutor five of her less talented classmates, Kirishima had teased his volatile friend, saying "That's what *virtue* looks like."

"I've got virtue too. I'll tutor you 'til you're dead,"

had been Bakugo's retort. Kirishima, ranked fifteenth in the class, held him to that.

Now in the library, Kirishima dropped his typically booming voice and asked, "Maybe we should've done this at home."

"Me? Make the trip to your place? No freaking way," replied Bakugo, making no noticeable effort to keep it down.

"What about your house, then?"

"And deal with my pain-in-the-butt hag of a mom? Pass. Let's just hurry up and finish this crap."

"Heck yeah! Ah, too loud. Sorry..."

Kirishima shrank, feeling the stares again. He'd never been much for libraries—the boisterous Kirishima and quiet places mixed about as well as oil and water. But if he wanted to attend the training camp, he had to learn this material.

"What's with the 'sorry, sorry'? You dumb or what? Oh, right. You are."

"I ain't dumb. Well, dumber than you, I guess, which is why we're here in the first place."

"Only gonna explain stuff once, so pay attention."

"Heck yeah, I will! Ack."

"Just show me the damn problems already."

"Right. First… This."

Still aware of stares from other patrons, Kirishima brought out his textbook and pointed to the quadratic equations that had been giving him trouble.

"I'm kinda lost when it comes to math, man."

"This piss-easy stuff…?"

Bakugo looked at the first problem, thought for a moment, and dashed off the answer.

"There. Done."

Kirishima stared blankly before giving an uneasy laugh.

"Yeah, okay, but I need to know how you got the answer."

"How? Just work out the calculations like usual. You stupid?"

"Thing is, I don't even know how to start 'like usual.'"

"Huhh? All of math's just about this basic sort of calculating."

"Sure, so could you teach me whatever tricks you use for all that?"

"It's all baked right into the equation, don'tcha see?"

"No, I don't. So why don't you explain it, nice and slow..."

"Just multiply these guys, add these other ones, and bam."

Another blank stare from Kirishima, while Bakugo gave him a no-nonsense glare.

Still all Greek to me...

Kirishima clutched his head. He knew how smart Bakugo was. Smart enough to understand just about anything at a glance. Smart enough that he never really needed to study, to the extent that struggling with schoolwork was an alien concept to him.

"After smashing these guys together, you just take down these other suckers to solve it."

This was Bakugo at his most earnest. Kirishima listened to the nonexplanation, held back some tears, and managed a thumbs-up.

"That was a real manly way to put it, dude..."

"Huhh?"

At Kirishima's reaction, Bakugo's brow furrowed even more.

"You need me to teach you the freaking times tables?"

"I'm not that dumb, man!" shouted Kirishima, louder than ever.

A wave of shushing from the surrounding library goers turned the boy's face beet red with embarrassment. Bakugo was amused, for a change.

"Heh. You suck, and now they know it too."

"You're the one who brought up times tables!"

As Kirishima offered another series of hushed apologies to the onlookers, a wide-eyed boy clutching a picture book marched right up to the table.

"Huhh? What's this kid want with us?"

"You lost, little guy?" asked a concerned Kirishima. The boy shook his head, pointed at Bakugo, and spoke.

"He's the one who won the U.A. sports contest but then they had to tie him up at the end, right? Why'd they tie him up? Cuz he was so loud? If someone's being loud in the liberry do they get tied up here too?"

Bakugo had in fact won the U.A. Sports Festival, but such was his fury and indignation over the circumstances that he'd been bound in chains on the victor's stand. Now this child's innocent question reminded Bakugo how Todoroki—the runner-up—had in effect handed Bakugo the win by not giving it his all in the

final match. The last thread of his patience snapped.

"Shut the hell up, you brat!"

Bakugo's roar echoed through the library before Kirishima could react. Yelled at by a stranger for the first time in his life, the child's face crumpled, his eyes filled with tears, and he wailed, only adding to the cacophony.

"R-really, really sorry, everyone!" sputtered Kirishima as he leaped up and dragged his short-fused friend from the library.

UA

While the fate of Kirishima's training camp experience hung in the balance, Jiro was finally understanding those same tricky quadratic equations.

"I think I get how to solve these now."

"Yes, Jiro. It's easy to get stuck on this part, but once you see the problem for what it is, you'll be just fine," said Yaoyorozu.

"Only cuz you're such a good teacher, Momoyao!"

Yaoyorozu's digestible explanations were just what Jiro needed, so she meant every word.

"Me? Surely I can't take all the credit..." said the tutor, blushing and obviously pleased with herself.

"Professorozu! How do I translate this one into English?" yelped Ashido.

"Let's see, Ashido... Ah, of course..."

Yaoyorozu has formulated the perfect study plan. A thoughtful approach, with batches of questions tailor made to fit each tutee's abilities. Questions that targeted their weaknesses, implicitly designed to teach them counterstrategies. Though Jiro, Sero, and Ojiro had at first been flustered by the splendor of the Yaoyorozu home, realizing the lengths their friend had gone to had helped them to buckle down and focus. Ashido's major motivator? Getting to participate in the so-called test of courage during the upcoming training camp. The sixth member of the study party was another story, though.

"Ugh... My head's gonna explode..."

Kaminari had been so distracted by the Sports Festival and the internships during their first school term that any thought of cracking a book had completely slipped his mind.

"When X and Y form an ionic bond...the auxiliary

verbs that founded the Sumerian empire will..."

"Sounds like your brain's already busted," said Jiro, from the seat to the left of Kaminari. Though he hadn't discharged any of his trademark electricity lately, he seemed to be going into full-on babble mode. To the right of Kaminari, Sero chimed in.

"Pull it together, man! You wanna attend the training camp, right?"

"That's right. Remember what Aizawa Sensei said? Failing these tests means summer school hell," added Ojiro.

"Argh! Somebody... Can somebody spare me some brains?"

Faced with cold, hard reality, Kaminari seemed to burst and deflate all at once.

"Yikes. Sorry..." apologize Ojiro, his encouragement having backfired.

"Kaminari, everyone... Why don't we take a short break? Proper rest is crucial to the process."

Yaoyorozu paused, turned to the door, and said, "Uchimura?" The butler promptly opened the door and strode into the room.

"May we have some tea?"

"Certainly, miss."

Was he standing out there the whole time, waiting? wondered a wide-eyed Jiro.

Without delay, several maids wheeled in a cart with tea and cookies. The tea set was, naturally, classy beyond compare, and the wafting, steamy aroma told the kids that they were about to enjoy some fine black tea. Careful not to disturb this precious break time, Uchimura and the maids swiftly served the tea and exited the auditorium.

"Enjoy, everyone," said Yaoyorozu. At this, her five students put down their pencils and grabbed their teacups.

"Heh. Tea poured for me by a real-life maid..." mused Kaminari, the luxury of it all rejuvenating his weary spirit.

"Mmm, so relaxing..." said Ashido as she slumped down in her seat.

When Yaoyorozu paused between delicate sips, Jiro asked, "You said this was Harrods?"

"Yes, I'm quite fond of this blend while studying. It's multiorigin, with a complex flavor that somehow calms and refreshes tired minds..."

"Dunno what most of that means, but I know what I like," said Sero.

"And I don't usually drink black tea, but this stuff is pretty good," added Ojiro.

Ashido's eyes shifted to the plate of brown cookies and began to sparkle.

"These cookies look yummers, too."

Though slightly misshapen, the cookies resembled the fancy sort you might see at high-class patisseries, so the group began to dig in while Yaoyorozu watched, pleased as ever.

A rich, almost savory sweetness hit them, but only after a bizarre burst of bitterness. All five paused, puzzled by the evolving taste. Before they knew it, burning, acrid spiciness. Then, shocking saltiness. The barrage of flavors hit their tongues, filled their mouths, and ran down their throats. And the pièce de résistance was a raw, almost fishy aftertaste that invaded their nostrils.

These cookies were not fit for human consumption. The kids instinctively knew this, but the plush surroundings made them doubt their senses. Maybe this was the newest taste sensation among the rich and fabulous?

"Whatever could be the matter?" asked their host, noticing them turning pale, suppressing their gag reflexes, and breaking out into cold, greasy sweats before washing down the culinary mistakes with gulps of tea.

"Not to your liking, then?"

"W-what? Naww, they're great..." sputtered Ojiro.

"So this is how the other half eats. Wow..." said Sero.

At this, Yaoyorozu warily picked up a cookie for herself and took a bite. Her face contorted in shock at once.

"Erm... Pardon me. Be right back..." said Yaoyorozu, hands covering her mouth.

As soon as her footsteps were out of earshot, the dam burst and the other five started speaking their minds.

"Yechh, I can still taste it!" said Ashido between gulps of tea.

"Th-those aren't cookies... They're bioweapons," muttered Kaminari, eyeing the plate with intense suspicion.

Always looking on the bright side, Ojiro said, "At least we're wide-awake now. One bite was all it took."

"And a second bite would keep me up all night, if I were brave enough," added Sero in all seriousness.

Jiro drained her teacup and glanced at the door.

"Momoyao thought they were awful too, right? Isn't that why she panicked like that?"

"I bet she'll be back before we know it," said Kaminari.

He was wrong, though. Yaoyorozu did not return quickly, and although her students tried to start studying again, the absence of their teacher made a world of difference for their focus. What's more, Jiro suddenly found herself in need of a toilet, as the tea she'd guzzled to cleanse her palate of the cookie had run right through her.

"I gotta find a bathroom. Be back soon."

"Me too! After all that tea, y'know," said Ashido, leaping up to join Jiro. A maid awaited them on the other side of door, presumably standing by to address any and all needs. They asked for directions, and the maid told them to follow her. Ashido's bladder was near to bursting by the time they navigated the twisting hallways and at last arrived at the bathroom.

"Phew. Just in the nick of time," she said.

"Must be tough living in such a labyrinth," remarked Jiro.

The girls did their business, washed their hands, and emerged into the hallway, smiling.

"Hang on? Which way did we come from?" asked Ashido.

The hall extended seemingly without end in either direction, and they weren't sure whether to go left or right. The maid was gone. Dismissed, in fact, since Jiro had sheepishly assured her that they'd have no trouble finding their way back. Ashido thought for a second and started marching to the right.

"Feels like it was this way. C'mon."

"You sure?" asked Jiro, who wasn't at all sure.

UA

"What's taking them so long? Think they fell in? Or got lost?" cackled Sero.

Ojiro seemed genuinely concerned.

"Lost, maybe. Definitely possible in this house."

"Didn't they have a maid showing them the way, though?" retorted Sero.

"Oh. That's true," said Ojiro with a smile.

Nearby, Kaminari rubbed his head against his notebook, writhing in agony like some sort of giant grub. Unable to ignore the antics, Sero glanced over at Ojiro before turning to Kaminari and asking, "And what, dare I ask, is up with you, anyway?"

"Maybe, if I do this enough, the knowledge'll just soak into my brain."

"I think you might end up losing brain cells instead," said Ojiro.

Kaminari nearly leaped from his seat, on the verge of tears.

"Then what the heck'm I s'posed to do?"

"Just keep studying, like the rest of us!" suggested Sero.

"But my head's at full capacity, man! Can't fit another vocab word or equation in there! Ugh... It's farewell to awesome training camp and hello to summer school hell for me!"

The soothing effect of the maid-served tea had long since worn off for Kaminari. Not ready to abandon a friend in despair, Ojiro and Sero kept trying.

"Y-you'll be okay! There's still time to figure it out," said Ojiro.

Sero dug deeper and said, "Exactly! And there's nothing people can't overcome with good old-fashioned focus! Remember our school motto?"

"It's 'Plus Ultra'!" added Ojiro, backing up Sero.

"Even that had slipped my broken mind..."

There was no snapping Kaminari out of his doom and gloom. He was usually one of the most upbeat members of the class, but academics was the one thing that made him shift gears into negative mode.

"Plus Ultra is all you have to remember! The rest will follow."

"When Ojiro's right, he's right. You just gotta go the distance, and that spot at training camp is as good as yours!" said Sero.

His classmates' warm encouragement was just the oil Kaminari's jammed gears needed.

"Right! Plus Ultra will do the heavy lifting for me..." said Kaminari, lowering his eyes to the page of his English textbook. But all he saw were the twenty-six letters of the Roman alphabet arranged in seemingly

random jumbles. His last brain cell fizzled.

"Nope. Can't. Not happening!"

Unwilling to face reality, Kaminari slammed his head on the table, no longer capable of hearing his friends' pep talk. All that echoed through his mind was a certain suggestion made half in jest by Minoru Mineta a few days earlier.

"If it comes to it, you could always just..."

"Ha ha."

A dry laugh from Kaminari. When Mineta had heard about Yaoyorozu's study party, he'd offered an alternative.

"Hey man, are you really losing it?"

"If it's that bad, maybe you should head home and rest."

Sero and Ojiro thought the cram session might have actually made Kaminari crack, but he lifted his head and smiled painfully.

"Nah, I was just thinking... Mineta said that if Yaoyorozu couldn't help me, I could always just cheat."

"Ha ha, but if you got caught cheating, you could definitely kiss the training camp goodbye," said Ojiro.

"Yeah, that's no laughing matter. They'd probably

expel you for that," added Sero.

Laughing matter or not, all three boys found themselves chuckling nervously.

"Sure. Right," said Kaminari, now staring at his friend's elbows—the source of Sero's tape, courtesy of his Quirk. It was a versatile Quirk, as Sero could launch the tape long distances and use it to drag things back to him. Kaminari found himself picturing the class's seating arrangement. Sero sat behind him, on the diagonal.

"Ha ha ha... Heh... Maybe that could work...?"

"Huh?"

Kaminari stopped smiling, and as his voice took on a deadly serious tone, Sero's and Ojiro's eyes grew wide with shock.

UA

"Perfect! I feel right at home in a noisy hangout like this! Right, Bakugo?"

"If you say so."

After fleeing the library, Kirishima and Bakugo had taken refuge at the diner in front of the station. Sunday

afternoon was past peak business hours, but the place was still packed with customers. Animated conversations filled the air, so the boys didn't stand out so much in this crowd.

A waitress walked over and asked for their order.

"The serve-yourself drink bar, with unlimited refills! For both of us!" answered Kirishima cheerily.

"Your treat, right?" questioned Bakugo, who was slumped down in the booth.

"You bet! Long as you take this tutoring seriously!"

"You think I can be bought with a few drinks? As if."

"The drinks are just over there, boys," said the waitress with a service industry smile. She left, and Kirishima shot up.

"I'll get the drinks. What're you having?"

"Cola."

"You got it, bud!" said Kirishima, heading for the drink bar.

Bakugo wasn't alone for long, though, because another customer spotted him and walked over.

"If it ain't Katsuki!"

UA

Coming back with the drinks, Kirishima noticed that Bakugo had been joined by two other boys—one with black hair rife with cowlicks and another with long hair parted down the center. They were chatting with Bakugo as if they knew him.

"Never thought we'd run into you here, man."

"Hey, we saw you in action at the Sports Festival!"

"Ugh, just shut up already!"

"Friends of yours, Bakugo?" asked Kirishima.

"Oh, another U.A. kid," said Center Part, noticing Kirishima standing over them.

"Yeah, we hung out back in middle school. Now hurry back to your own table, you two," spat Bakugo bluntly.

"Oof. Icy cold, man."

The pair reluctantly stood up to leave, but the grinning Kirishima had other ideas.

"Naw, sit back down, guys!"

"Huh? You sure?"

"Of course. I bet you three have plenty to catch up on?"

"No. We don't. What about your studying?" seethed Bakugo.

"Not even for a few minutes? Why not? You gotta treasure the friends you've made, dude!"

"What the hell? You seem, like, way too nice a guy to be friends with Katsuki," said Cowlicks, practically blinded by Kirishima's noble aura. Both Bakugo and Kirishima responded at once.

"What's that s'posed to mean, you?"

"Bakugo may have a bad attitude and a nasty mouth on him, but he's a man's man who's just following his convictions!"

Bakugo swiveled toward Kirishima and glared.

"Don't start in with that mushy crap, broomhead!"

"Yup. Same old nasty mouth, it seems. Even when someone's complimenting him," said Center Part, who seemed to be reminiscing. This got Kirishima curious.

"So what was Bakugo like in middle school, anyway?"

"Hmm... Pretty much just like this?"

"The most arrogant guy you ever met."

"Yeah, thought he was the center of the universe."

"You jerks looking for a beating or what?" said Bakugo, clenching his fists.

"What's this? A future hero is no more than a violent thug?"

"Shaddup! And outta my way, you extra."

Bakugo shoved Cowlicks aside and stomped off toward the drink bar to refill his glass.

"Actually, he almost seems to have chilled out a little since middle school," muttered Cowlicks, once Bakugo was out of earshot.

"Yeah. Maybe?" agreed Center Part.

"Back then, he seriously would've hit us for saying that crap. And he wouldn't have been caught dead tutoring someone."

"For sure. U.A. must be something special to change him like that... So? How's Katsuki behaving nowadays?"

Kirishima thought for a moment.

"Like I said earlier, I guess? What you see is what you get, which is why I like hanging out with the guy. Plus, he's got real talent. Everyone can admit that, at least."

As Kirishima talked, he thought back to the early

days of the school year, when he and Bakugo had first met. Even more than now, Bakugo had been angry and sharp-tongued, with every other word out of his mouth either an insult or a threat. He'd had it in for Midoriya, especially.

"Hey, putting two and two together, you both must've also been in the same class as Midoriya, right?"

Cowlicks and Center Part glanced at each other and mumbled, "Well... Yeah, actually."

Suddenly, Kirishima remembered how Midoriya had been when they'd started school at U.A. The guy had an awesomely powerful Quirk, but he was always hurting himself because he couldn't quite control it yet. In contrast, he was earnest almost to a fault and strangely lacking in confidence.

"We knew Katsuki was a shoo-in, but Midoriya? Getting into U.A.? Not in a million years..."

"Why's that?"

Cowlicks forced a smile and scratched his head like he had something to hide.

"Truth is, we picked on Midoriya, like, all the time... We thought he didn't have a Quirk, see."

"So when he revealed all that power? I was like,

'Whoa.'"

"Seriously. We saw the whole Sports Festival on TV, and we had goose bumps when he crossed the finish line in first place. That was just nuts…"

"Yeah…"

There was a note of regret in their voices. Something uncomfortable about their expressions, too. Kirishima had no patience for those who were mean-spirited, and he didn't understand what could lead someone to pick on others. At the same time, he wasn't about to lecture people who clearly felt remorse over what they'd done. That was up to the one who'd been bullied.

"I bet Midoriya would love to hear that! He'd probably be blushing like heck right about now," said Kirishima.

Midoriya looked up to All Might in every way, so he was definitely the type to laugh it off and forgive these boys. He might not even think of it as forgiveness, since to him, helping those in need came as naturally as breathing.

"Uh-huh. Probably," said Cowlicks.

"He was always a decent guy," added Center Part.

The two seemed relieved, and they started talking a

mile a minute, as if a great weight had been lifted from their hearts.

"Anyway, don't tell Katsuki I said this, but Midoriya was on fire in the tournament too! In the battle against that, uh, icy dude!"

"Never could've imagined Midoriya duking it out with someone, but there he was. He sure showed us."

"Right? When he fired back after that one hit, I was like, 'Holy crap!'"

"Gah, Midoriya came so close! We might've seen an insane battle between him and Katsuki if he'd made it to the final round!"

"What's that about Deku?"

The three boys spun around at the sound of Bakugo's voice. Their friend was back, drink in hand, with one eyebrow twitching furiously at a dangerous angle.

"An insane battle? Deku? Keep the fan fiction to yourself! You blind or something? Maybe a few good explosions'll get you seeing straight again!"

"Cool it, Bakugo!" implored Kirishima.

"Once you all shut the hell up, sure!"

"Same old Katsuki, huh… At least when it comes to Midoriya!"

"Don't you freaking say his name!" screamed Bakugo.

"Relax already, Katsuki."

Center Part and Cowlicks scrambled to escape Bakugo's fists while Kirishima tried to get between them all. In the process, the table rocked and sent a glass to floor, where it shattered. Bakugo's anger was past the point of pacifying, and the other diners were starting to stare.

"That one boy looks familiar..."

"Ah, he's from U.A.!"

"And that business with the sludge villain?"

"They had to restrain him at the Sports Festival."

"Yeah, he's the one."

The whispers from the peanut gallery were just more fuel to Bakugo's fire.

"Shaddup! You extras need to pipe down and keep shoveling that crappy slop into your grub holes!"

"Excuse me, sir."

The hand that clamped down on the shoulder of the screaming Bakugo belonged to a stern-looking staff member. Her name tag identified her as the manager.

"I'm afraid you're disturbing the other guests, so if

you could keep the noise level down..."

If words alone were enough to quell Bakugo's rage, the world would be a more peaceful place indeed.

"Buzz off! I'm a guest too, y'know!"

"A guest who bothers other guests is no guest of ours. And we do not serve 'crappy slop' at this establishment."

As expected, Bakugo and the three caught in his orbit were kicked out of the diner.

"This's cuz you jerks just *had* to bring up Deku! Hang on... It's all Deku's fault, really!"

"You gotta calm down, Bakugo!" pleaded Kirishima, doing his best to restrain his friend.

"Gr-great catching up, I guess!" said Cowlicks as he and Center Part fled the scene.

It made Kirishima think. Maybe Bakugo had chilled out a little since the start of the year. Midoriya had gained some confidence, too. That said, it might take a while before Bakugo's short fuse actually got any longer. Might also be a while before the books and pencil case in Kirishima's bag saw any real use.

U/A

While Kirishima was finding the resolve to do his own studying, Jiro and Ashido were still lost in the mansion.

"I never should've dismissed the maid like that..." said an increasingly desperate Jiro.

"Still, we're bound to find our way if we walk long enough," said Ashido, who still wore her Pollyanna smile.

"Not like we get this sorta opportunity every day! Why not explore while searching for the auditorium?"

"Huh?"

"Explore! It's an adventure!"

Ashido was practically skipping at this point, with Jiro plodding along close behind.

"Ooh, maybe Momoyao will even show us her room later."

"Yeah. Maybe..."

There were endless identical doors on either side of the winding corridors. Jiro felt validated about her use of the word *labyrinth* earlier.

What's it like actually living here?

It must be nothing special to Yaoyorozu, though, as she'd grown up here. Jiro was suddenly reminded of Mamayao's withering stare, and she glanced down at her outfit again.

"Hey. Anything weird about my clothes?"

"That getup? Naw, it's awesome! Hmm? This must be the library!"

Ashido oohed and aahed over the plaque next to a conspicuously large door, and Jiro let out a small sigh. She and Ashido had similar tastes. One might divide them into slightly different cliques, but they belonged to the same genre, so to speak. Yaoyorozu, though? On another planet altogether. If Jiro's fashion was punk, Yaoyorozu was (rich) girl next door. Rock versus classical, in music terms. Their hobbies, looks, and home lives couldn't have been more different, to the point that their gender was just about the only thing they had in common. Despite this, they'd somehow become friends.

Yaoyorozu was, in all respects, a good girl. She had perfect looks and was always trying her darndest, even if she sometimes lacked confidence. She wasn't stuck-up at all and was easy to talk to. Jiro hoped their friendship would continue to blossom, of course, so it was painful to imagine being judged by Yaoyorozu's family.

"Ah, there you are, Miss Jiro, Miss Ashido."

"Oh. Mr. Uchimura…"

Jiro turned to find that the butler had nearly snuck up on them. Maybe he'd followed the sound of Ashido's whoops and cries?

"So terribly sorry. I was sure I asked one of our staff to escort you…"

"Ah, not the maid's fault. I told her not to bother."

"Be that as it may, it is our duty to ensure you don't become lost, and in that, we have failed."

"Don't sweat it! We had a little fun exploring," said Ashido, reassuring the butler.

"I see. Very well… Back to the auditorium, then…?"

But Uchimura paused in place and thought for a moment.

"Actually, perhaps we could pay a visit to Miss Momo?"

The two girls followed the butler, and a bizarre smell soon wafted toward them. The smell grew stronger as they walked.

When she could no longer stand it, Ashido held her nose and said, "Yeesh, what is that?"

Uchimura stopped and spun around.

"The cookies you were enjoying earlier, miss."

"Eh? That fits, I guess."

"Please, this way..." said Uchimura, urging the girls onward. They were practically tiptoeing as they approached their destination at the end of the hallway.

"Mother, please... I don't think that's a good idea either..."

"And why not?"

Jiro and Ashido could hear Yaoyorozu and Mamayao. They peeked through a crack in the door.

"It's just that sardines and chocolate are hardly an ideal pairing..."

"But, Momo, the fish's omega oils are good for the brain. As is cacao. Don't worry—once we blend it all together with the oysters, you won't even recognize the fish. They were in the earlier cookies too, and I bet you couldn't tell."

It was a fully equipped kitchen like you might see in a restaurant, and mother and daughter were standing in front of a counter that was covered in fresh fish, cabbage, spinach, a variety of nuts, spices, and many more ingredients. The girls in the hallway gleaned that the cookies that had nearly killed them earlier had been Mamayao's doing.

"I take it Mamayao's not the greatest cook, huh," whispered Ashido.

Jiro nodded at her friend's assessment and thought about it.

Unexpected in all sorts of ways, though... That her mom would even try to cook, I mean... And be so into it?

Unaware of her eavesdropping friends, Yaoyorozu kept pleading her case.

"But the fishiness it adds... Can't you smell how bad it is, Mother...?"

"Hmm? Come to think of it, no, I don't smell a thing. Perhaps I've caught a cold?"

You'd have to chop off your nose not to smell that...

Or maybe Mamayao had just grown immune after too much exposure to the vile odors, Jiro thought.

"Why not take a break, then? You've been working so hard, Mother."

"Nonsense. I can't afford a break. These cookies won't bake themselves, after all."

Why go to so much trouble, though?

Jiro couldn't imagine, but Mamayao, with clenched fists, had an answer.

"These are for your friends and their final exams, Momo! Failure means not attending training camp, yes? Since you're kind enough to tutor them, the very least I can do is provide a few batches of brainpower cookies for the study party."

Jiro gasped and took another glance at the ingredients on the counter. Sure enough, every last item was one type of "brain food" or another.

"Mother... I really, truly appreciate the sentiment, but..."

"It will be fine. Yes, I may have mixed up the salt and sugar last time, but not again. What's more, this green tea will neutralize any offensive odors. Or should I use curry powder instead? Well, let's toss in both to be safe!"

Huh. She's a totally relatable mom.

Jiro reflected on this. Whether in a tiny apartment or an enormous castle, any good mother would be eager to make cookies for her daughter's friends. Tastiness not guaranteed, of course.

"Aww, Mamayao's such a sweetheart!" cried Ashido.

Jiro nodded, and Yaoyorozu finally noticed her friends.

"What are you two doing here?"

"I brought them, miss."

The butler stepped forward and gave a slight bow. Jiro wondered if he'd purposely planned to have them learn the terrible secret behind the inedible cookies.

"You two, um, really don't have to eat these cookies..." whispered Yaoyorozu. Considerate as ever, she was wary of hurting her mother's feelings.

This family is totally normal after all.

Jiro somehow felt relieved by this and chuckled.

"Don't worry. The flavor was...unique, let's say, but probably just the boost our brains needed, right?"

"Yeah!" added Ashido. "Perfect for getting us into study mode!"

"On that note, let's get back there and stuff a few more down Kaminari's throat, okay?"

Yaoyorozu stared at her friends for a second before breaking out into a wide smile.

"Then we had better bake up this next batch, yes? We'll even prepare an extra-large cookie just for dear Kaminari."

"Good idea," replied Jiro.

At this, Mamayao stopped bustling and stared at Jiro's clothes for the second time that day, causing the girl to squirm.

She must really have something against my outfit...

"I must say, I love your fashion sense."

"Say what?" Jiro blurted out, not believing her own elongated ears.

"I apologize if my staring came off as rude! It's just, back in the day, a friend in the grade above me was in a band and wore clothes just like yours. Seeing your outfit brought back those memories..."

"But, Mother, didn't you attend an all-girls school?"

"Yes. This friend was a bit of a tomboy, but one admired by all. I tried copying her style for a time, but I could never quite pull off the look... Ah, how nostalgic."

Mamayao was suddenly a blushing schoolgirl again.

"Was that all?" asked Jiro, almost let down.

"I'm so sorry, Jiro. I hope you weren't offended..." said Yaoyorozu in earnest. Jiro smiled.

"Nah, the opposite, kind of."

"How do you mean?"

"I thought I'd offended *her* somehow."

Yaoyorozu cocked her head, clearly puzzled. Behind her, Mamayao gasped and said, "Ah, of course. I nearly forgot the cake!"

Jiro's eyes bulged as Mamayao extracted a beautifully decorated chocolate cake from the massive refrigerator.

"Wow, pretty..." said Ashido.

"Um, did you make this, Mamayao?" asked Jiro, warily.

"No, I had our chef prepare it, so you can be sure it's scrumptious."

Yaoyorozu dropped her shoulders in obvious relief and said, "Why don't we enjoy this cake and then get back to work?"

"Work, yeah! But first, cake!" agreed Ashido, leaping into the air. Yaoyorozu and Jiro glanced at each other and grinned, while Mamayao and Uchimura beamed at all three of the girls.

"Y'think they're still studying back there?" asked Ashido.

"I certainly hope they are. Especially Kaminari..." answered Yaoyorozu.

"Those slackers? I'd put money on 'not,'" said Jiro.

The three girls arrived back at the auditorium, ahead of the cake.

"Psst. Let's surprise them!"

At Ashido's suggestion, they opened the door a crack and peered inside. No apparent slacking off—the three boys were deep in serious conversation.

"Plan C is all about that single moment. Boom or bust," said Kaminari, sounding beyond serious.

"The problem is the noise, right? Somebody's sure to hear," said Ojiro, grimacing.

"I know!" said Kaminari. "Maybe get someone in the Support Course to whip you up a tool, Sero? Like a silencer."

"A silencer, huh. That could be all kinds of useful..." said Sero, giving the suggestion real thought.

A cabal of villains formulating an evil plot wouldn't have sounded as dastardly as these boys.

"What on earth are they talking about? What's 'plan C'...?" whispered Ashido.

"New costumes, maybe?" suggested Jiro.

"It hardly feels right to burst into the room at the moment..." said Yaoyorozu.

None the wiser to the girls' presence, the boys kept discussing.

"There're a few big issues. First, how to silence Sero's tape. Then, the timing between me and Sero... Finally, how to destroy the evidence in case this whole thing goes sideways. Sure wish we could use Ashido's acid for that."

Ashido gasped at her unwitting involvement in the scheme, whatever it was. Clearly Kaminari wanted to use Sero's tape for something or other, but why destroy the evidence?

Oh. I get it.

No sooner had Jiro figured it out than Kaminari nodded confidently and said, "Perfect. This'll get me to that training camp for sure... Plan C... C for 'cheating,' that is!"

"Come again? Please tell me I heard that wrong, Kaminari!"

"Buh?! Momoyao!"

The boys spun around at the sound of Yaoyorozu's shout, and all color drained from their faces. The plan, of course, had been for Sero to write the test answers on his tape and pass them to Kaminari. Jiro had guessed right. Next to her, Ashido puffed out her cheeks in anger.

"Destroying evidence with acid, huh? What, and make me an accomplice to your dirty little C? You guys suck!"

"I knew you were dumb, but this dumb, really? Actually, I expected better from Ojiro and Sero," chided Jiro.

"I'm ashamed..." admitted Ojiro.

"B-but Kaminari turned all serious, so we just sorta got roped into it, and..." said Sero.

With the walls closing in, Kaminari pleaded, tear ducts about to blow.

"But I just can't learn any more! Cheating's the only way I'll ever pull it off!"

He hung his head low, and Yaoyorozu crouched to meet his gaze.

"Kaminari, tell me—did you have to cheat to get into U.A.?"

"N-no way! I mean, it was a close call, but I passed that entrance exam fair and square!"

Yaoyorozu responded to Kaminari's desperation with a hard stare.

"Then I'm sure you can manage this, too. You're quite capable when you put your mind to it. I truly believe that!"

"Ohh, thank you, Professorozu!"

The would-be teacher's warmth and compassion melted the icy shackles around her pupil's heart.

What the hell?

Jiro had had enough of this exhausting melodrama, so just in time, Kaminari dried his eyes and returned to the table with renewed conviction.

"I'll put in the effort, Teach! Just you watch!"

"That's the spirit, Kaminari!" said Yaoyorozu.

"We're gonna beat this thing together, yeah!" said Sero.

"Training camp for everyone! And don't forget the test of courage!" said Ashido.

"At the very least, let's hope nobody fails," said Ojiro.

Laser focused on the training camp, the group of six was once again united in spirit, and the study party continued. Jiro contributed by stuffing one

of Mamayao's cookies down Kaminari's throat, as promised.

Before long, they'd all have that sweet, sweet cake.

Part 2
Bumpy Ride

"Class A's bus is this way. Please line up in order!"

Tenya Ida, president of class A, was in top form as he corralled his classmates toward the bus parked in one of U.A.'s lots.

"Beautiful day, huh!" remarked Izuku Midoriya, adjusting his camping bag on his back. Shoto Todoroki's blasé reply was, "Guess so." He had nothing against Midoriya—this was just his usual energy level.

"Thanks a lot for teaching us and stuff, Professorozu!" said Mina Ashido.

"What she said! And how about another study party come winter term finals?" added Denki Kaminari.

"If you think I can be of assistance, then yes,

absolutely!" replied Momo Yaoyorozu, to the two tutees who had needed her help the most. Kyoka Jiro couldn't help throwing a jab Kaminari's way.

"Try cracking a book yourself next time, Kaminari."

"Ugh. Always kicking a guy when he's down, huh, Jiro?"

A few paces away, Tsuyu Asui stared at Ochaco Uraraka's bag.

"Packing light, Ochaco?"

"Yeah, nice and compact is what I was going for. Your bag's huge, Tsuyu!"

"The biggest one we had at home. Big enough to fit me in there, even."

This was the first day of training camp. In telling his students that those who failed their final exams would miss the camp and have to endure summer school hell, class A's homeroom teacher Shota Aizawa had perpetrated another of his so-called rational deceptions. This one had been designed to give some of the kids the kick in the pants they needed. All had passed the written exams, but Kaminari, Kirishima, Ashido, and Rikido Sato had failed their practicals. Hanta Sero and Minoru Mineta's duo had technically

passed, but since Sero had been immediately put to sleep by Midnight's Quirk during the exercise, he'd received a failing grade. All five would be attending supplementary lessons during the camp, which was simply hell by another name. Still, the entire class was ready to attend a week of training camp.

Though Uraraka and a few others lived on their own while attending U.A., most still lived at home with their parents. Needless to say, the prospect of a week in the great outdoors without parents had them good and stoked. There was also the matter of Midoriya encountering the League of Villains' Tomura Shigaraki at the mall just a few days prior, which had prompted a last-minute change of location for the training camp, for security reasons. This only added to the class's desire to escape the anxieties of everyday life and leave it all behind for a spell.

"Our bus is over here. Hurry up."

Class B's president, Itsuka Kendo, herded her class-mates toward their own separate bus.

This training camp was to be a joint exercise for the two first-year classes of the Hero Course—A and B. Though Neito Monoma, Tetsutetsu Tetsutetsu, and a few other class B students had sparked rivalries with their class A counterparts at the Sports Festival, the two classes didn't interact much, so this was yet another factor throwing electricity into the air.

"The 'B' must stand for 'bountiful babe buffet'..." muttered Mineta as he ogled the class B girls boarding their bus. Though he didn't actually make a move, his drool and heavy breathing alone bordered on sexual harassment—all par for the course for this embodiment of lust.

"Mineta! That is class B's bus. You need to line up over here!" shouted Ida, not noticing what was drawing Mineta's attention. The class president's reprimand ended the boy's momentary fantasy, and he reluctantly joined his classmates.

"Now then, we will sit according to our seating chart in class!"

Ashido groaned at Ida's demand.

"Do we gotta, really? Why not just sit wherever?"

"But going by the standard arrangement will make the process quicker and more efficient, no?"

"C'monnn, it's not every day we get a training camp trip! Why make it extra boring on purpose?"

"Ashido. This trip is an official school function, so

I'm afraid your boredom is irrelevant to the matter."

"I wanna sit wherever, too!" said Kaminari, backing up Ashido.

Ida thought for a moment.

"Shall we take a vote to decide?"

"Just get on the bus already," said Aizawa from behind, before anyone could respond. He had the final say, and the students of class A rushed onto the bus without another word. Aizawa hated wasting time more than anything—a fact that his students knew all too well.

It was a standard tour bus with five rows of four seats each, two on either side of the aisle.

"Wanna sit with me, Ochaco?" asked Tsuyu, seeing Uraraka glance around.

"Yeah! Definitely!"

The class streamed onto the bus.

"I want a window seat!"

"Ugh, whose bag is this blocking the aisle?"

"The seats way in the back… That's where the baaad kids sit, yeah?"

"It doesn't matter where you sit, just sit."

Aizawa's gravelly voice once again brought the commotion to a swift end.

U·A

The bus engine rattled to life. By the time the scenery was flying by, Aizawa's authority had all but evaporated.

"Let's have some music! Something summery! Some Tube songs, maybe!" said Kaminari to his front row seatmate, Kirishima.

"No way, nothing beats Carol's *End of Summer* in the summertime!" said Kirishima, scrolling through his phone for tunes.

"But it's not the *end*."

On the other side of the bus, also in the first row, Ashido and Toru Hagakure played a game.

"Your turn!"

"I spy a bank!"

"I spy money in the bank!"

The class was as wild and carefree as a group of kindergartners on a field trip. Aizawa—sitting in front of Hagakure—was about to blow his top when the presidential Ida stood up and shouted from his seat behind Kaminari.

"Quiet down now, everyone! Didn't you read the

pamphlet for this excursion? Including the reminder to always respect the rules, as we are at all times ambassadors for U.A.?"

But Ida's voice was drowned out by the din. His own seatmate, Midoriya, grabbed his shoulder gently.

"Th-that's all right, Ida. Besides, you probably shouldn't stand up while we're moving."

"Hmph! How careless of me!"

Oh, whatever, thought Aizawa, giving up on any hope of disciplining his class and deciding instead to catch forty winks. He knew that all the chiding in the world wouldn't keep the noise from rising up again, like the immortal phoenix, and he needed to conserve his energy and sanity if he was to survive a full week of cohabitation with these kids. Besides, this would be their last chance to get it out of their systems.

As Aizawa settled into his nap, Asui offered Uraraka a thin red box.

"Want some Pocky, Ochaco?"

"Sure do!"

"Give me some Pocky as well, *oui*?"

"Here, Tsuyu, I brought candy too!"

"Thanks."

"Hey, I said give me some Pocky," repeated Yuga Aoyama, peeking through the seats in front of the girls. Todoroki sat to his left, behind Ashido.

"Whoa, Aoyama!"

"I didn't expect you to be a fan of Pocky, Aoyama," remarked Tsuyu as she slipped the box between the seats, allowing Aoyama to grab one of the chocolate-covered sticks.

"*Merci*," said the boy, flipping his hair for no apparent reason. "I was up late last night packing and overslept. No time for breakfast, you see, so this Pocky will have to suffice. ☆"

"'Suffice'? Kinda rude to the Pocky, don'tcha think?" said Uraraka. "It's the ultimate harmony between pretzel and chocolate!"

The frugal Uraraka was keenly aware of the value of things—hence her impassioned defense of such a luxury item. The candy she shared with Asui had been part of a care package from her parents.

"As you say, mademoiselle."

Upon finishing his stick of Pocky, Aoyama extracted a compact mirror with sparkly decorations from his pocket and began checking himself out from all angles.

 **MY HERO ACADEMIA** SCHOOL BRIEFS

"You mind?" grumbled Todoroki, who'd been blinded by reflected sunlight.

"Sorry, ☆" said Aoyama, shifting closer to the window, still not quite done with his mirror.

"I must sparkle more than the morning sun, even. ☆"

"You're something else, Aoyama," said Uraraka.

"In an almost impressive way. Almost," added Asui, nodding at her friend.

Behind them, Bakugo and Fumikage Tokoyami had their eyes shut, as uninterested in the music, games, and antics as their teacher. Bakugo was already fast asleep, while Tokoyami was meditating in an attempt to drown out the world around him. The seats behind them held Mashirao Ojiro and Sero, with Mineta and Sato to their left, across the aisle.

"Ashido's not the only one excited for this 'test of courage' thing! Can't wait to try scaring people," said Sero.

"Or sneaking up from behind and grabbing their boobs!"

"That's technically a crime, Mineta," said an exasperated Ojiro. Next to Mineta, Sato unfolded a delicate paper package.

"Want some marshmallows, guys? I've got vanilla, chocolate, and strawberry."

"Only if marshmallows is code for boobs!" quipped Mineta, who only ever had one thing on the brain. In front of them sat class A's taciturn twosome, Mezo Shoji and Koji Koda. Shoji broke the silence.

"Koda."

"Y-yes?"

"Want the window seat?"

"No, I'm okay here, actually..."

"Right. Sure."

Their entire row—the one with Bakugo and Tokoyami—fell back into silence.

"Momoyao, wanna listen? I've been hooked on this band that does arrangements of classical stuff," asked Jiro in the next row up.

"My, that sounds fascinating."

"We can listen together, then," said Jiro, handing Yaoyorozu one of her earbuds.

"What's up, Tsuyu?"

Asui had poked her head above the seat to scan the rest of the bus.

"Nothing. We've been driving awhile, is all," she said before sitting back down next to Uraraka.

"Yeah, I hear you. Kinda exciting, though, going on a trip with everyone! I swore I'd keep awake and chat the whole time, but now I'm getting sleepy..."

"Where'd you go for your big field trip in middle school, Ochaco?"

"Tokyo! It was great living the dream for a few days. How about you, Tsuyu?"

"Hokkaido, of all places."

"Ooh, nice! I hear they've got good crab up there."

"The crab was tasty, but... Ribbit," said Asui, a froggy chuckle escaping her lips.

"Hmm? So good you're laughing just remembering it?"

"Nuh-uh. I had this friend named Habuko, you see, and she couldn't stand the cold. Worse than me, even.

She was as excited as anyone for the trip, but the closer we got to Hokkaido, the drowsier she got…"

"Yikes. Nothing you can do about the climate, I guess."

"But she still wanted to enjoy herself, so we came up with a way to keep her awake."

"Yeah?"

"She just needed to keep warm, right? So we borrowed a bunch of clothes from our classmates for her to wear."

"And? Did the strategy work?"

"Yes, but by the end, she was practically a snowman with all those puffy layers. She'd never looked cuter."

"Sounds like you made some good memories!"

"Uh-huh," said Asui with a grin, just before a reflected beam of light shot into her eyes from between the seats in front of her.

"Too bright, Aoyama."

"Oui…"

But this wasn't the typical, enthusiastic *oui* they'd come to expect from the boy. Uraraka and Asui glanced at each other before peeking through the seats.

"You okay, Aoyama?"

"Ughh…"

A pale Aoyama was draped against the wall of the bus, head resting on the windowsill. One limp hand still clutched his compact mirror.

"What's the matter?" asked Uraraka. Todoroki had been listening to Midoriya and Ida's conversation, but at this, he turned and noticed the state of his seatmate.

"Something wrong?" asked Todoroki. Midoriya and Ida also glanced over.

"Probably motion sickness, from staring into that mirror all this time?" proposed Asui, but Aoyama took a deep breath and fired back.

"My beautiful visage could never make anyone sick, least of all *moi*… ☆"

With his whole body trembling violently, he managed a weak wink.

"We applaud your brave face, but you really need to take it easy," said Asui, not beating around the bush.

"*Non, non*… I will be…just fine… Urp."

Sensing what might be coming, Uraraka yelled, "Anyone got a barf bag?"

"Someone as beautiful as myself would never do such a thing… And if I did, even the barf would surely twinkle… Urrp."

The rest of the class paused their own conversations and took notice.

"Eh? Aoyama's gonna hurl?"

"How awful!"

"You okay, man?"

"Sick from staring into a mirror? You idiot!"

"He reaps what he sows…"

While commentary poured in, Asui calmly gave advice.

"Let's get that window open, first. Then loosen your shirt collar and try to lie down."

"Got it," said Todoroki, taking charge. He stood up, cracked the window, and raised the armrest between him and Aoyama. After undoing the top button of his uniform, Aoyama said "Merci… ☆" and lay down, per his doctor's orders.

"I can, um…switch seats with you, Todoroki!" offered Midoriya, but Todoroki declined. Instead, he crouched and flipped open the extra aisle seat. It was smaller than the capacious standard ones, with nothing in the way of back support.

"That's not gonna work for you, Todoroki!" laughed

Ashido, seeing the boy awkwardly perch himself on the tiny platform.

"Not even a little!" agreed Hagakure.

"I don't think these seats were designed to 'work' for anyone," said Todoroki flatly.

Midoriya couldn't take it, though.

"C-come on, Todoroki. Just switch with me! I'm smaller, after all!"

"Nonsense. As class president, this is my burden to bear!" said Ida, who was now standing and engaging in one of his strange habits—swinging one of his arms wildly.

"No way, Ida! You're practically the biggest one here!"

"But, Midoriya, the president must always be ready to suffer for his class! Why, I could even get by performing air chair!"

"Air chair? So can I!" said Midoriya, fighting back.

Seeing these two squabble, as if each were insisting on paying the bill at a restaurant, Todoroki stood up and laid his hands on their shoulders.

"It's fine. Really. I have a place to sit, and that's good enough."

"Right. And what matters now is that Aoyama starts

feeling better," pointed out Asui, which convinced Midoriya and Ida to sit back down. Todoroki took his new seat too. Up in the first row, Kirishima—still looking at his phone—had an idea.

"Says here there's a pressure point that can help when you're carsick! Just press the spot two fingers' width down your wrist."

"Let's try," said Todoroki, volunteering for duty. But as he reached for Aoyama's arm, Todoroki shuddered and froze up.

"Wait. No. Not me..." he muttered, all eyes on him. Todoroki stared intently at his own hands and held his breath, as if about to confess to murder.

"When I get involved, people's hands end up destroyed..."

"Huh?"

"I'm the hand crusher..."

Most of the kids had absolutely no idea what Todoroki was mumbling about, but Midoriya and Ida burst out laughing. Their friend had made a similar remark when all three had found themselves hospitalized in Hosu City after battling the Hero Killer, Stain. Ida had suffered permanent damage to one of his hands during the attack, and Midoriya had mangled his own hands when he'd fought Todoroki during the Sports Festival. The common element was Todoroki himself, so he was particularly wary about hurting other people's hands now, even if Midoriya and Ida took it as a joke.

"I just can't... Someone else needs to press your pressure point."

"I can do it myself, merci. If everyone could just leave me be, actually..." said Aoyama.

"Also... It might help if we distracted the patient somehow!" offered Kirishima, still reading off his phone.

"I know just the thing," said Ashido. "Let's go in order and play the word chain game!"

At her suggestion, Midoriya started muttering like mad, mostly to himself.

"That might be perfect, actually... It's a simple game on the surface, but thinking up words does require some focus. Since each subsequent word has to start with the final letter of the last one, your options are more limited than you'd think. And no time for deep thought, right? Because the other players are pressuring you to hurry up. That sort of mild stress activates

the brain cells and trains the mind... Two birds, one stone."

"Haven't heard Deku's wacky muttering in a while!" said Uraraka with a wide smile.

"Eh? Oops, sorry," said a blushing Midoriya.

Ida stood up and faced the back of the bus.

"On that note, attention, everyone! Our friend Aoyama is suffering from motion sickness, so we will be playing the word chain game to keep his mind otherwise occupied!"

"The word chain game?" said Mineta, clearly not thrilled about the idea.

"What're we, in grade school?" mocked Sero.

Ashido shot back.

"Yeah, the word chain game! It's also the perfect way to kill some time!"

"No, Ashido, this is for dear Aoyama's sake! But also perhaps a way to practice cooperating as a class, in light of the impending training camp!"

Ida's insistence got the rest of the class on board.

"All in agreement? Very well. To give our ailing Aoyama time to think, let's begin from this side of the bus, with Kaminari, then Kirishima, myself, Midoriya, and so on."

"Okay," said Ashido. "What's our starting word?"

"How about *training camp*, so Kaminari's gotta start with *p*!" proposed Hagakure.

Kaminari thought hard for a moment.

"*Perturb*. As in, what Mamayao's cookies did to my stomach."

"My turn!" said Kirishima. "*B*, huh? Let's see… *B*… *B*… *Bulletproof*!"

"*F*… *Footwork*! An obvious choice, for me," said Ida.

Midoriya was up.

"*K*… Hmm… Oh, *Kamui Woods*! Names are allowed, right?"

"You sure do love your heroes," quipped Todoroki.

"That would make my letter *s*, I suppose. Well, I do enjoy reading and studying, so how about *scholar*," said Yaoyorozu with a reassured nod. Next to her, Jiro furrowed her brow.

"*R*… *R*… Ah, how about *reggae*? Pfft…"

"What's so funny, Jiro?" asked Yaoyorozu.

"Just thinking how, when Kaminari goes into

dummy mode, his favorite music genre's probably 'regg-yayyy.'"

"You never miss a chance to take a shot at me, huh," grumbled Kaminari, peeking over his seat at the laughing Jiro. Farther back, Shoji spoke.

"My turn... *E*... *Extremity*, then."

Fitting, as Shoji's Quirk was "Dupli-Arms." It was now the animal-loving Koda's turn.

"*Y*... *Y*... *Yaks*...?"

"Like the animal? Not what Aoyama's about to do?" said Sato. "Lemme see... So I got *s*... *Spoom*!"

"The heck is that?" asked Mineta, unfamiliar with Sato's chosen word.

"A dessert! Kinda like sorbet, but lighter, and served in a glass. Usually made with fruit juice, or even fruity alcohol."

On the other side of the bus, Tokoyami muttered "Fruit? Like apples...?" though nobody heard him.

"Fine, fine, my turn," said Mineta. "You gave me *m*, so... *Misandry*. For all those man-hating women out there."

Mineta started gnawing on his nails, prompting his seatmate, Sero, to ask, "Seriously, man, what did Mt. Lady do to you during that internship?"

"I might just tell you, but only if you're ready to never trust females again…"

"You know what? Never mind. Anyway, I've got *y*, then? Umm… *Yuca!*"

"Yuca?" asked a dumbfounded Ojiro, who was up next.

"Never heard of yuca? It's a tropical tuber, kinda like a potato. Real healthy, though, with manganese and vitamin C, which boosts the immune system, keeps your heart pumping, and even prevents wrinkles," explained Sero, clearly in his element.

At the mention of wrinkle prevention, Hagakure yelped, "Ooh, I'd better eat some yuca, then!" Her Quirk made her completely invisible, but the girl was still, for some reason, obsessed with skin care.

"You sure know a lot about it…" said Ojiro.

"What can I say?" added Sero. "I'm all about healthy foods."

"Almost seems unfair, using a word nobody's heard of."

"Heh. Word chain game is a battle of wits, and I've come well armed," bragged Sero.

Ojiro narrowed his eyes at the cackling Sero and started to think of his own word.

"*A…* Oh, *ant!*"

"C'mon, that's so ordinary. Boring, even," said Sero, feeling let down by Ojiro's choice.

"What's wrong with being ordinary...?" mumbled Ojiro with an expression of pure angst.

From the next seat up, Tokoyami gave the two boys a silent stare.

"Your turn, Tokoyami," urged Ida, since Tokoyami was staying quiet.

"Your letter is *t*, Tokoyami," said Asui, peeking back between the seats.

"*Twilight*," said Tokoyami, but only because the others wouldn't leave him alone until he played along. Uraraka was impressed, at any rate.

"Ooh, perfect word for you. Next is...Bakugo. Wait, is he sleeping?"

Bakugo was indeed dead to the world, so Sero reached around and jostled him.

"That takes guts..." murmured Midoriya from his seat up front, obviously impressed with Sero's bravery.

"Bwuh?"

Bakugo's eyes popped open.

"Your turn, man. We're playing the word chain game."

"And your letter is *t*, Bakugo. Got that? *T*!"

All eyes were on Bakugo, and his own eyes narrowed dangerously.

"Huhh? Word chain?"

"Yes. You got *t*," repeated an unafraid Uraraka.

"She's got guts, too..." repeated Midoriya, drawing Bakugo's attention. Whether it was the sight of Midoriya's face that did it or not, Bakugo's blood pressure spiked.

"Trying to rope me into your stupid game for babies? Buzz off!"

"Not exactly a word, but good enough. So my letter is *f*," said an unshaken Asui.

"Wait! What? That wasn't me joining in! Don't make me part of this!"

But Bakugo was now part of this, and the class moved on.

"I think I know what your *f* word is gonna be, Asui..." said Uraraka.

"You're expecting *frog*...? Just to mix things up, I'll go with *flag*."

"That still leaves me with *g*! Okay... Hmm... *Gouda*! It's not mochi, but cheese isn't all bad," declared Uraraka.

Asui peeked over at Aoyama and said, "It's your turn. And your letter is..."

"Urrp..."

Aoyama was as pale and limp as ever.

"Still not feeling well, huh... Why don't you take your turn, Todoroki?" suggested Asui.

"Fine... Hmm..."

Todoroki fell into deep thought, scowling, unaware of all the eyes on him. Then, in a flash, he raised his head.

"*Hypothermia.*"

"But gouda ends in *a*, not *h*, Todoroki! That means the game's over," said Midoriya.

"Aww, I didn't get to go!" said Ashido from the next seat up, clearly annoyed.

"Oh. Sorry," was Todoroki's rather unconcerned apology.

U

"Why don't we restart the game, beginning with *a*?"

"But, Ida, maybe this isn't the best game for poor Aoyama? We need something that can keep his mind occupied the entire time," suggested Asui.

"Hrm. You may be right," said Ida with an overly profound nod. "How about a quiz, then?"

"Yeah, right on! Quizzes and bus trips were made for each other."

Kaminari's enthusiasm brought a confident smile to Ida's face.

"As I am class president, I will come up with the quiz questions. Aoyama will be given the first chance to answer, and if he fails to do so, the question goes to the rest of you! On that note, question one... Factor the following: $(x - 1)(x - 2)(x - 4)(x - 7) + 16$."

"Not that kinda quiz! None of us wanna be doing homework!"

Ida was taken aback at Kaminari's protest.

"But we are high schoolers, are we not?"

"In this setting, a quiz is more like...trivia! Y'know, fun stuff! Give him an example, Midoriya!"

"Eh, me? I-I dunno..."

Midoriya wasn't quite ready for this sudden responsibility, but he immediately started thinking.

"Okay, let's start simple… Way back when, All Might was doing a live segment for the TV show *Passionate Planet*. In the middle of shooting, a dog ran into the road, and All Might saved it from getting run over. What was that dog's name?"

"How would literally anybody know that besides All Might himself?" said Uraraka, poking fun at Midoriya. He squirmed, clearly embarrassed.

"I assumed everyone knew nearly everything about All Might… My other questions were gonna be 'How many times did All Might say the words *I am* in his *Heroes Monthly* interview three years ago?' and 'What color was his necktie when he did the photo shoot for that interview?'"

"Nope. Nobody knows any of that stuff," said Kirishima.

Midoriya's eyes grew wide. "Eh? Really? You guys weren't counting the number of times he said *I am*? You didn't take note of his outfit?"

"You're the biggest All Might fanboy here, Midoriya," added Asui.

In Midoriya's mind, "fanboy" was just another way to describe someone following his dreams. Feeling like the others had recognized his love for All Might, he chuckled and blushed.

"She didn't mean it as a compliment, you goddamn nerd!"

Seeing his childhood playmate's awkward smile was more than enough to light Bakugo's fuse. Or maybe he was always lighting it himself, subconsciously?

"Aoyama, do you remember the dog's name?" asked Ida, wanting to move on from the volatile reaction between Midoriya and Bakugo.

"Non... I never knew it to begin with..." said a weary Aoyama, hair flapping in the breeze from the open window. Near his feet, Todoroki looked up at Midoriya.

"Was it Pochi?"

"So close! Ponta, actually!"

"All right. That's enough of this sorry excuse for a quiz," groaned Kaminari.

U.A.

A voice from the back row.

"None of you have a clue how to go about this, huh?"

Everyone turned to look at Mineta.

"You need a way to keep a man distracted? Then open the floor to me."

"Better not be some pervy story," said Jiro with a scowl. Yaoyorozu backed her up.

"Yes. Nothing vulgar, please."

"All I'm talking about is a way for a guy to keep his mind off things!"

"Sure, except your mind and mouth have taken up permanent residence in the gutter!"

"Yeah, that's right!"

Mineta's expression showed his utter contempt for the girls shouting him down. Meanwhile, Ida stood up and turned toward Mineta, hoping to cut the confrontation short.

"Listen to reason, Mineta! We're inside a bus, so I'll ask that you not force others to listen to these stories of yours!"

"Please, President... I'm a man who knows his audience. There's a time and place for everything, right? And what? Is this suddenly a dictatorship?"

"Of course not! I have the utmost respect for everyone's views and opinions!"

"Then it's not really fair for you to cut me off before I've even started, right?"

"Hrm... I suppose not. Very well. Let's hear what you have to say."

Always striving to be fair and just, Ida had been cowed by Mineta's sophistry, triggering another round of outcries from the girls. Most of the boys were silent, with a few secretly looking forward to whatever was coming.

"This was back in elementary school, yeah? There was this video rental place, and they'd just stopped me from peeking at the R-rated corner for about the hundredth time..."

Mineta wore a queer expression as he started his story, and Sero couldn't believe his ears.

"You've been like *this* since elementary?"

"A perv right outta the womb!" cried Ashido from the front row.

Mineta snorted and retorted, "Ha! You call that perverted? I'm just getting started! Anyhow, I was walking home from the video store, and near the riverbank in my neighborhood, a piece of paper flew past my feet. White, standard size... It wasn't from a dirty mag, so I was gonna just keep on walking, but something told me to check, just in case. So I picked it up and turned it over, and the back was covered in all this writing. Couldn't read most of the kanji since I was so little, right? Still, I could sense it was something special."

"How? What'd you sense, exactly?" asked Mineta's seatmate, Sato.

"What can I say? This piece of paper was just oozing with *passion*. Anyway, I brought my discovery home, keeping it secret, and whipped out a kanji dictionary to help me decode the writing... *Debase*... *Slobber*... *Impurity*... Turned out to be a page from a novel about a young widow who starts selling her body to pay back her dead husband's debts..."

"Not exactly proper reading material for a little kid," said Ojiro with a pained look. Mineta snorted again.

"Don't be dumb. The gates of literature are open to

people of all ages, no?"

"Yeah, but that definitely sounds like erotica," said Jiro, not hiding her disdain for her classmate. Another snort from Mineta.

"I prefer to call it an amorous novel! Listen, porn and steamy lit are as different as can be. Like sun and moon! An electric range and a roaring bonfire! If porn is your basic Turkish bath, then fine literature like this is a hot springs retreat in the mountains! It's the difference between fast food and a seven-course meal! It's like…"

Mineta was a man on a mission, and the metaphors kept coming until Shoji produced a mouth at the end of one of his dupli-arms and spoke.

"We get it. Calm down."

"Of all the stupid…" growled Bakugo, looking like he'd swallowed something bitter. As he attempted to fall back asleep, his seatmate, Tokoyami, said "Agreed" and shut his eyes for another round of meditation. Paying them no mind, Mineta resumed his tale.

"So, like anyone would, I wanted to know the rest of the story. I ran down to the riverbank the next day and found a bunch more pages, all scattered around. When I

started picking 'em up, though, this middle-aged home-less dude shambled over and said, 'Give those back...' I was like, 'No way, they're mine now!' and ran home with everything I'd found."

"Huh? What if the book really was his?" asked Ashido.

"That'd make you a thief," said Kirishima.

Mineta brushed off the accusation with a big wave of one of his tiny hands.

"Just keep listening... I got home, got out the dictionary again, and kept reading. The sexy young widow discovers her hidden talent for pole dancing and quickly rises to the top of her field. Along the way, she has a fling with a waiter, gets into catfights with her fellow dancers, and agrees to be the club owner's mistress... Until that relationship blossoms into true love..."

"Huh. Didn't expect that."

"I like where this is going, actually..."

The girls had been only reluctantly half listening, but their ears pricked up at *true love*, since they were at just the right age to go gaga over romance, even more than over sweets. Mineta surveyed his audience haughtily, knowing they were good and hooked.

"So then the club owner wants to help the widow escape her sordid life, right? But the waiter goes crazy with jealousy and rats them out to the manager, who— BLAM—shoots the club owner dead... The boss makes the widow *his* mistress, and she gives in to lust as a way to forget the death of her true love."

"I know the feeling! When times are tough, you gotta cling to whatever you can!" said Hagakure, nodding wildly.

"I'll never forgive that darn waiter..." said Uraraka with all the subdued fury of a wronged protagonist in a kung fu film.

"Hang on, the boss of what, exactly?" asked Kaminari.

"As their affair gets hotter and hotter, the boss actually starts to fall for the widow. Yes, true love blossoms in his heart..."

Mineta put extra feeling into his retelling, making Jiro cock an eyebrow.

"Eh. What's with all this blossoming love?"

"No, I totally get it! Men are pure souls too, deep down!" shouted Kirishima, raising a single clenched fist. Mineta went on.

"But she doesn't understand this change that's come over the boss. She thinks he's just gotten sick of her, so she starts seducing every man she lays eyes on. Tells them to do whatever they want to her, as a way of punishing herself..."

"No! Don't do it, girl! Have some self-respect!" cried Kaminari, finding it painful to imagine the widow's further descent into debauchery.

"But then someone unexpected shows up to lend the widow a hand..." continued Mineta with gravitas. Most of the bus was turned toward him by this point, listening with rapt attention.

"Yeah?"

"Go on! Who was it?"

But their expectations were betrayed, to the last.

"Well, I ran out of pages right around there."

"Argh! I gotta know what happens to the poor widow!" blurted out Kirishima, in spite of himself. The audience was hanging on Mineta's every word now, and his smug smile only made them more curious.

"So I went back to the riverbank to find more pages. Searched 'til my eyes were aching, but no dice, since it'd already been a few days since I found the first part of the story. The homeless dude was still there, though, and he handed me a single page. 'Looking for this, are you?' he asked. It was more of the book, and it turned out this guy was actually the author."

"No freaking way!" said Kaminari, practically leaping from his seat at this shocking twist.

"The homeless guy had always wanted to write erotica for a living, but he had only ever done it as a hobby since he didn't have the courage to go public. One day, though, he came out and told his family that he was gonna become that sort of author. They were totally against the idea. Unable to stand their lack of support, the man left home and started living by the riverbank. That was about a week before I happened to walk by."

"Walking out on family is hardly the mature thing to do," said Yaoyorozu. "One must face reality before one's dreams can come true."

"C'mon, don't be so harsh," said Mineta. "When his family stood in the way of his dreams, this guy lost all his confidence. He basically gave up on everything and threw down the book he'd been working on, which was when the winds of fate blew the pages around and sent one flying right to my feet. I told the guy all this and explained how his book was so pervy—I mean,

fascinating—that I'd looked up all those kanji in the dictionary just to read it!"

"And there we go. Pervy. Like I said," quipped Jiro, right on cue. Mineta ignored her.

"The dude started crying tears of joy, hearing how excited I was about his story. 'So don't you dare give up on your dreams,' I told him, and he called me a little knucklehead. In the end, I asked him to keep writing stories, cuz I'd promise to read them all and love every word... I also asked him to add more detailed descriptions of boobs, if possible!"

"Knucklehead? He wasn't wrong, there," said Sero. Mineta ignored that jab too.

"He swore he'd keep trying, shook my hand, and then we parted ways. Must've gotten his mojo back, since about a year later, he made his big debut as an up-and-coming erotica author."

"Wow! How about that!"

"One of his books is about to get turned into a direct-to-video movie, even! Man, I can't wait 'til I'm old enough to check out the R-rated section of the video store."

Upon hearing that the man had achieved his dream,

the whole bus was left feeling somewhat warm and fuzzy. But Kirishima was puzzled.

"This whole story wasn't actually…that pervy…?"

"True… Almost something wholesome about it…in a weird way…" agreed Midoriya.

Some of the other boys made odd faces, like the story had given them indigestion.

"Hang on!" said Hagakure. "How'd the book about the widow end?"

Mineta's face filled with animalistic lust, his eyes bloodshot and his mouth curling into a disgusting sneer.

"Heh. You really want to know? Then drop by my place, and I'll show you my signed copy, if you know what I mean."

"Ugh, you're the worst!"

Another round of boos from the girls, but Mineta—wearing that same provocative sneer—accepted it all as a badge of honor. He lifted a soda to his lips and drained the whole thing, like a celebratory toast to himself after a hard-won victory.

"How're you feeling, Aoyama?" asked Asui, checking in on her patient.

"Worse than ever, I'm afraid..."

Mineta's story hadn't distracted him from his woes at all, but Asui nevertheless decided to take a similar approach.

"How about a story from me, then? This one had my little brother on the edge of his seat."

"Ooh, let's hear it, Tsuyu," said Kirishima, his curiosity piqued. Asui nodded, paused, and began.

"This happened when I was young. It was my first trip to stay with a cousin in the countryside. My big sister—two years older than me—took me out to play. We splashed in this shallow brook, hunted for cicadas, and played hide-and-seek in the sunflower fields."

"Sounds amaaazing," said Uraraka, beaming, as the description conjured an idyllic, pastoral tableau in her mind. The rest of the bus seemed to breathe a sigh of relief too, since Asui's story was already sounding more pleasant than Mineta's.

"At some point, another girl about my age came by

and asked if I wanted to play with her. *The more the merrier*, I thought, happy to have a new friend. My sister remembered something she had to do, though, and headed back to the house without me."

"Whoa, she just left you behind, Tsuyu?"

"The house wasn't far, and my new friend and I wanted to keep playing. She seemed to have all the energy in the world, and before we knew it, it was sunset. I told her I had to get back, but she wouldn't have it."

"Kids can go on playing forever, if you let 'em," remarked Kirishima, nodding. But a stern look came over Ida.

"Wouldn't your late return cause your family members to worry?"

"Of course. Which is why I told her that we could play again the next day, but that only made her cry. So I agreed to stay out a little longer. She was so thrilled that she decided to bring me to her secret spot—a place filled with fireflies, apparently."

"Fireflies... So magical..." cooed Hagakure, spellbound. This caught Aoyama's attention.

"I shine brighter than any common firefly..." said

the boy, still trembling like a newborn fawn.

"Oh? Aoyama speaks!" said Ashido, glancing at the seat behind her.

Any reference to things that shone, glittered, or sparkled were sure to get a rise out of Aoyama, so Asui's story was already more interesting to him than Mineta's. Asui waited until the chatter subsided and went on.

"She took my hand and led me up the mountain, along this little winding path, and through a small red torii gate. It was getting dark by that point, but I had my new friend, so I wasn't scared. After a while we arrived at her secret spot, and as promised, there was wave after wave of fireflies dancing through the night. Almost like a rain shower of pure light!"

"Sounds amazing!"

The kids could picture the verdant mountainside, covered in ghostly orbs of light, each its own little moon condensed to a point, flickering in and out of existence. An illuminated dance so enchanting one might forget to blink while gazing in awe. The listeners imagined the scene with their own imaginative touches, captivated by the story. Even Aoyama, still trembling, spoke up.

"I too am like a shower of light…"

Asui surveyed her audience and took a breath before continuing.

"I honestly don't know how long we stood there, taking in the beauty. In any case, when I heard my cousin calling me, the two of us ran back down the mountain. I thanked my friend for showing me her secret, and laughing, she said, 'Make sure it stays secret.' It was ours, and ours alone. Before long, we made it down to my cousin, and my sister was also there, crying her eyes out. She asked, 'Were you out there playing alone all this time?' 'No,' I said, 'I was with her.' But when I turned to point to my new friend, there was nobody there."

At this final line, everyone's faces froze, and a pall fell over the bus.

"I thought that maybe she'd run off on her own, but my sister had no memory of the girl. She said it'd just been the two of us playing, earlier."

"You don't mean…? No way…"

"I learned that for years there'd been cases of children getting spirited away in the area. Maybe the ghosts of children who'd died on the mountain were

looking for friends? My sister was furious. She said I'd probably been seconds away from being snatched up and turned into a firefly myself... And when we went back to search, the next morning? The little path and the red torii gate were gone. Where did I really go that night, I wonder...?"

Asui's typically detached tone suddenly took on an edge of terror.

"Eek!" yelped Jiro.

"Yikes, no way!" said Hagakure.

"If you're gonna tell a spooky story, you gotta let us know from the start!" protested Uraraka. These three particular girls couldn't stand scary stuff, and the color had drained from some of the boys' faces, too, when the story had taken a turn from wholesome to terrifying.

"Great. And right when we're about to camp in the woods..."

"I can't do mountains, man... Don't wanna get grabbed by the ghouls..."

"Oh? Was it that scary? My little brother loved this story," said Asui matter-of-factly.

"All right, quiet down. The bus is about to stop," growled Aizawa, who was good and awake now. The whole bus hushed, like a classroom at the chime of the bell.

UA

The bus pulled over, but the turnoff had no rest stop, no bathrooms, nothing. Just mountains as far as the eye could see, not a building in sight.

"Get off now. Hurry up."

At Aizawa's urging, the kids started to get up, assuming this would be a brief pit stop to stretch their legs. Mineta fidgeted, in dire need of a bathroom after gulping down all his soda.

"Ughh…" said Aoyama, struggling to lift himself up.

"Well, Aoyama? Did my story help to distract you at all?" asked Asui.

"Not in the least, as I twinkle far brighter than any firefly…"

As he spoke, he brought out the mirror again and began to fix his hair.

"Right. Well, I admire your dedication to personal grooming, even when you're queasy."

"This is the only way I know how to be... Hmm? Hmm...?"

Still staring into the mirror, Aoyama bobbed his shoulders up and down and put one hand to his stomach.

"You good, Aoyama?" asked Ashido, noticing the change.

"Why, I seem to be cured. ☆"

He was looking less pale, and his trademark wink had regained its sparkle.

"Maybe because the bus stopped moving?" wondered Asui with a tilt of her head. Aoyama flashed his usual smug smile and wagged a slender finger side to side.

"Non, non. It is because I have viewed my own beautiful visage. ☆"

"Ugh. We were seriously worried, man."

"I'm taking back my sympathy."

The other kids were slightly irked at Aoyama's miraculous recovery, and they made it known as they filed off the bus. Aoyama got off too, in his own detached, devil-may-care way. Hearing the others complain, a croaky laugh escaped from Asui.

"What's up, Tsuyu?" asked Uraraka.

Asui found it all so charming. The word chain game, the quiz, the stories... Even the complaints directed at Aoyama were just proof that they all cared.

"Just thinking about how sweet everyone is."

It hadn't been even half a year since school had started, but the class had already spent plenty of rich, quality time together. This bus trip had revealed yet another side to their dynamics, and Asui was looking forward to the training camp to see what else might be revealed.

"I said, hurry," grumbled Aizawa at Asui and Uraraka, who were the last ones to get off. They gazed up at the endless sky, marveled at the far-flung mountains, and sucked in the fresh air. The forest spreading below the turnoff was a dense, brilliant green. No, the members of class A—who were still thinking of this as an easygoing field trip—couldn't possibly have imagined the trial that would await them just minutes later. Training camp would begin sooner than they knew.

The boy slipped through the tiny door into the dim space and calmed his breathing, as if melding into the darkness itself. What came next could make or break the plan. He'd run this simulation in his head hundreds of times, and failure at this point would send all the dominoes crashing down. Quick wits and cool-headed judgment would be key.

The damp earth beneath his feet was still warm, unwilling to relinquish the last bit of heat from the blazing sun, earlier. Or maybe it was his own heat the boy felt, penetrating the ground. At this thought, a bemused smile rose on his face. It made him keenly aware of his own nerves and inexperience, so he paused to collect himself and control the heat radiating from his body and mind. This plan had to succeed. If that meant an untimely death, he'd welcome the grim reaper with a smile.

From between the towering walls on either side, the boy could hear the rustling of the trees in the cool night air and the light lapping of water. Nothing more. This told him that nobody was beyond the walls at the moment. This moment would not go to waste, though.

He felt the inner lake of his spirit grow still, like a mirror's surface. From now on, no wasted motions to disturb the water. He reached into his baggy clothes and—ever so gently—brought out a small hand drill, whose tip he pressed against a spot on one of the wooden walls, at eye level. The metal ate away at the wood with a whirr that echoed loudly between the walls, but the boy did not panic or falter. Any hesitation now would mean he wasn't worthy to begin with. No, a life's worth of resolve had led him to this moment.

The feedback against his hand changed as the drill punched through. Penetration. The boy felt the heat rising in him again, and he fought to suppress it. He reminded himself that this plan demanded absolute caution.

Like the smallest ray of faint sunshine between heavy cloud cover, a thin beam of light crept in through the newly opened hole, half a finger's width in diameter. To the boy, this beam represented the stairway to heaven, for the source of the light was, to him, paradise.

He swallowed hard and placed the drill on the ground. Body trembling with excitement, he pressed his body to the wall and peeped through the hole. The view? A steamy *rotenburo*, or open-air bath. The peeper? None other than Minoru Mineta, class A's embodiment of lust. The plan? What else, but to spy on the ladies' half of the rotenburo.

Mineta had been anticipating this day, this plan, since before school had even started. No, to hear him tell it, base instinct had prepared him for it since before he'd been born.

The female figure gave Mineta life. It was his reason to exist. A haven in which men could find sanctuary and solace. A home to return to, without worries or cares. But for Mineta, the door to this particular home was shut fast. He would pound away at it, begging to be let in, but security at the door had an innate mistrust of the boy. The more he pounded and the louder he begged, the more suspicious he seemed, until his status changed from mere "suspect" to "criminal."

But *quit* was not in Mineta's vocabulary. If they wouldn't admit him into the home, the logical work-around would be to peer in from the outside.

Yesterday, the first day of training camp, was when he had stepped up to make his greatest wish come true. With sky-high expectations and operating purely on autopilot, he had attempted to scale the wall from the men's side of the rotenburo. The wall was actually two walls, though, and waiting for Mineta at the top, between the walls, had been Kota Izumi. The Catnip Inn was managed by the Wild Wild Pussycats (a hero team specializing in mountain rescues), and Kota was the young nephew of Mandalay, one of those heroes.

The goal of this training camp was to prepare the students to test for their provisional hero licenses, which would permit them limited Quirk use, even if only in emergencies. U.A. students wouldn't typically take the exam until early in their second year, but given the increased villain activity, the school had

decided that this crop of first-years had better be allowed to defend themselves.

Today's menu had consisted of brutal Quirk training starting at 5:30 a.m., but just as those with sweet tooths always have room for dessert, Mineta had plenty of stamina left if it meant going after women. The double-layered wall was an unexpected obstacle, to be sure, but Mineta had been preparing for this since the end of final exams. He'd picked the lock of the door leading to this space between the walls and had brought the drill to create the all-important hole.

In light of Mineta's failed peeping attempt the day before, the adults had seen fit to stagger the boys' and girls' bathing times. The boys of classes A and B had already enjoyed the rotenburo that night and were now engaged in some other nonsense inside the lodge, so no one would come looking for Mineta. This was his chance.

He stepped away from the wall, shut his eyes, and waited. No sense in staring through the hole in anticipation, unless he wanted his eyes as dried out as his teacher's often were. Better to save his strength for the greatest sight of his life.

A slender strip of sky was visible directly overhead. It was a velvety black—unlike in the city—with a dazzling number of stars, like so many shards of jewels and gems. The rustling of the trees, the hoots of owls, the earthy scent of the ground, the permeating presence of insects all around—Mineta took it all in, becoming one with the summer night.

On the verge of enlightenment, Mineta heard the sweetest sound he could imagine in that moment—the sliding of the door connecting the indoor bath to the rotenburo. At nearly light speed, his eye was pressed to the hole. Shock and horror! The steam from earlier had billowed and spread, whipped by the wind, enveloping the scene in white.

Damn steam!

Mineta cursed the steam to hell for ruining his view of heaven. Still, he could make out a few faint figures.

"Ooh, I love a good rotenburo."

"The perfect thing to rest one's weary soul."

"Mhm."

He analyzed the voices instantly.

Itsuka Kendo, president of class B.

Ibara Shiozaki, whose Quirk was "Vines."

Yui Kodai, a girl with a black bob cut.

A few more voices joined the mix. Yes, Mineta was after the class B girls. He'd thought it wise to switch targets, since the girls of class A were on guard after his failed attempt the previous day. Mineta had a high opinion of the class B girls as well. Nothing lacking there, so to speak.

"Huh? You've got a scratch on your back, Yui," said Kendo.

"Hmm?"

"Oh dear. Perhaps one of my vines brushed you earlier... I'm so very sorry!" said Shiozaki.

"Uh-uh." That was Kodai, likely shaking her head as if to suggest, "Don't worry about it."

Mineta could just picture the girls gazing at each other's naked backs within the steam.

"You've actually got quite a pair on you, Ibara."

"Do I really?"

"Mm-hmm. They say they'll grow even bigger with a little massaging. Want me to try?"

"*Oh my…*"

This girl-on-girl exchange played out only in Mineta's mind, though, as his fictional portrayal of paradise. Mostly, he wished he could somehow transform into a girl and insert himself into the fantasy. But no. Mineta snorted in indignation and composed himself. The actual women just beyond the wall didn't need any help from his imagination.

"Fwooo!"

He puffed his cheeks and blew into the hole with all his might, hoping to carve a path through the steam. Blow and peep, blow and peep, over and over. To Mineta, no effort was too much to ask for this prize. The blowing left him red in the face, head spinning, but the steam had begun to give way. Mineta spotted some bodies approaching and immediately forgot about his spinning head. At this rate, they'd come into clear view soon, steam or no steam. He stopped breathing and opened one bloodshot eye so wide it might have fallen clean out.

But then, voices he didn't expect to hear.

"Oh? There's a hole here…? Better plug that up."

"But first, a little *punishment*."

A familiar shock, as if from a pair of EKG paddles, penetrated Mineta's eyeball.

"Gahhhh!" he screamed, as the amplified sound of Kyoka Jiro's heartbeat was transmitted into his body via his eye. They'd never take him alive, though. He could still run while they lacked any evidence of his crime. He toddled toward the door between the walls, but his pursuers were not so easily thrown.

A sickly sizzling sound.

Liquid oozed through the drilled hole and began to melt away the wall. Mina Ashido's acid worked fast, and she was just as quick to pounce on Mineta. It wasn't only Jiro and Ashido, though—every girl from class A and B was present and accounted for.

The brief exchange between Kendo, Shiozaki, and Kodai earlier had been no more than a ruse to throw him off guard, and the "steam" was actually the product of dry ice, created by Momo Yaoyorozu's Quirk to block Mineta's vision.

"Alas, we were right to be cautious," lamented Yaoyorozu.

At her side, Kendo said, "Yeah, thanks a bunch!"

"Peeping is unacceptable, Mineta!"

"You're really gonna get arrested one day. You know that, right?"

"Ah, the little creep brought a drill and everything! This was totally premeditated."

As the girls closed in around him, Mineta gave up all hope of escape, and his expression warped in rage.

"Wearing clothes into the bath is against the rules!"

"Huhh?"

Of course the girls were clothed. No need to come naked to a sting operation.

"I don't even approve when they wear towels into the hot springs on travel shows!"

He didn't regret his actions one iota, and Mineta's egregious complaint lit the girls' fuses immediately.

"You...are...the freaking *worst*!"

"The only one breaking the rules is *you*!"

"Oh? I'd be happy to strip down and show you the goods if that's what you really wa—"

A massive palm came swinging at him before he could finish. Kendo's Quirk, "Big Fist," hit him with the force of a truck, and Mineta's world went black.

UA

"Ugh?"

Mineta awoke to find Ragdoll's round eyes staring at him.

"Aha ha ha ha ha! You back with us? Hey, Mandalay! Pixie-Bob! He's up!" shouted Ragdoll over her shoulder. Mineta surveyed his surroundings and quickly realized he couldn't move, bound as he was by ropes that wouldn't budge.

"No, you're not going anywhere, I'm afraid. Eraser told us to show no mercy," said Mandalay sharply.

"If you'd told me there were high school boys out there going around drilling holes to peep at girls, I wouldn't have believed it," cackled Pixie-Bob, half-amazed, half-disgusted.

This snapped Mineta back to reality. He remembered getting caught and then smacked unconscious.

Still can't believe them, violating those holy grounds like that! The bath demands fully stripped bodies!

Even caught and bound in ropes, Mineta was Mineta. He snorted at the unfairness of it all and glanced

around the room, spotting a desk and a sofa. The lodge's office, apparently.

"Well, might as well take our turn, now?"

"Yeah. Can't wait to wash off this sweat and grime."

"Bath time, yes!"

Hearing the three Pussycats' conversation, Mineta gasped and gazed up. The ladies were still in their hero costumes, and from below, Mineta could only see a great pair of mountains bulging from each of their chests.

Why climb the mountain? "Because it is there," said a great mountaineer, famously, and Mineta would have agreed. Mineta harassed because the boobs were there. And for that he could go to hell, as far as his female classmates were concerned.

Upon noticing Mineta's line of sight, Mandalay let out the sort of weary sigh that comes only with maturity. Meanwhile, Pixie-Bob grinned and said, "What, want to join us? Kidding!"

"Don't tease the boy. Now, Mineta—you're going to sit tight right here until we're done with our bath," explained Mandalay.

"We're locking you in here, too."

"See ya later."

With that, the three Pussycats left the room and locked the door, as promised. As soon as their footsteps faded, Mineta started squirming. He would never slip free...or so it seemed, until the ropes just fell away. Like the lock picking, escaping from ropes was another skill Mineta had mastered for just such an occasion. His eyes fell on a paper clip on the desk, and with a little more magic, he had the office door open. He snuck down the hall silently and escaped into the night air. Nearby, the outer wall of the rotenburo stood tall, but Mineta quickly scaled it with his "Pop Off" Quirk and landed inside the rotenburo area. No walls could keep Mineta out when his lust was in control.

"Plus Ultra," he muttered under his breath, like a grizzled action hero.

Nobody was bathing just yet. They must've still been in the changing room, getting undressed. Mineta breathed a smug sigh, pleased with this newfound success. More than at any other moment so far, this respite while waiting for the ladies to undress was deeply satisfying, and it filled him with hope. He was suddenly

in the mood for a nice cup of black coffee, or some equally suave way to pass the time.

And this time? Not mere schoolgirls, but grown women. At the thought of those mountain ranges, Mineta's mouth curled into a goofy grin. The bigger the mountains, the more worthwhile the climb. And if he could summit a pair of peaks at once, he could die happily right then and there. In the back of his mind, Mineta recalled Pixie-Bob's words.

"Want to join us?"

The "Kidding!" that had followed had been conveniently deleted from his memory bank.

Or maybe she'd said, *"Ooh, would you like to, umm, join us?"*

The version of Pixie-Bob in Mineta's mind suddenly turned bashful.

"Please, join us."

Now it was a request.

"Join us, and we'll show you a good time, I promise."

Now just as lusty as Mineta.

Mature babes all the way!

His far-fetched interpretation of Pixie-Bob's earlier teasing sent a torrent of blood rushing to Mineta's head and gushing straight out his nose. It splashed against the flagstones, covering them in enough red to suggest a murder mystery at the hot springs.

In his head, he and Pixie-Bob were already bathing together. Her two mountains would rise above the steam. Her slick skin would brush against his. *"No fair, Pixie-Bob. Let us get in on that action,"* Mandalay and Ragdoll would say. Scrambling to compete for access to Mineta, the three women would surround him with boobs. An abundant, bountiful, beautiful buffet of boobs. There'd been a coup over the central government of Mineta's mind, and it was now ruled by boobs. As if in some absurdist tale, he imagined waking up one morning to find himself transformed into a giant, sentient boob. While the visions played out, Mineta's feet guided him to the door leading to the indoor bath.

UA

He peered through the glass. It was steamy inside too, but Mineta could make out the hazy silhouette

of someone by the washing station, evidently washing their hair, based on all the shampoo bubbles. While Mineta had been dreaming of boobs, Pixie-Bob must have come in and started to wash up.

"You sure kept me waiting, boobs..." he whispered as he stripped off his top. The rules of this sacred space demanded nudity, after all. Mineta slid the door open gently and slipped into the bath. He was batting one thousand on this covert mission, so far.

"Hmm hm hm."

Some cheery humming was coming from the washing station. It sounded a bit deep and muffled for Pixie-Bob, but Mineta assumed it was just the acoustics of the space. The figure was now covered in bubbles, head to toe. Pixie-Bob must be the type to save time by washing everywhere at once, Mineta supposed. All the bubbles made her look twice her usual size.

Or maybe she's into bubble play. Heh heh.

Still ruled by desire, Mineta's mind leaped for the fetishistic interpretation.

Well, bring it on! he thought, knowing with absolute certainty that there was a real live woman hidden under the bubbles. Unable to resist his urges, he lunged toward the homecoming he'd long been denied.

"Boooobs, I'm hooome! Hmm?"

Instead of reaching around from behind and landing on a woman's chest, Mineta's stubby arms and tiny hands smacked up against a broad back. An incredibly muscled back. A pair of powerful hands grabbed ahold of him.

"Ohh? Who's brave enough to join me for bath time?"

"Eek!"

It was the fourth member of the Wild Wild Pussycats, Tiger. As an extra precaution, Mandalay and her two female colleagues had decided to bathe on the men's side.

Every instinct told Mineta to run, but he was thrown to the floor and pinned by a leg as thick as a tree trunk. Dumbfounded, he could only watch as the bubbles slowly slid off Tiger's body, revealing a smorgasbord of rippling muscles. Tiger was in fact a transgender man, though knowing that wouldn't have been much consolation to Mineta.

"Any last words, kid...?"

"All I ever wanted was to grope some boobs!"

"Maybe Datsue-bà will let you have a shot at hers!" roared Tiger, referencing the demon in the Buddhist afterlife who strips the clothes of the damned who are unable to pay for passage across the Sanzu River.

"Gahhhhh!"

Mineta's shriek echoed across the summer sky.

Part 4
A+B Slumber Party

"You hear something just now?" asked Toru Hagakure, curled up in her futon.

"Sounded like a boy? Screaming, maybe?" said Kyoka Jiro, cooling off by the open window.

"The boys were fighting at dinner, weren't they! With the class B dudes, I mean."

"Idiots. All of them... But no, this scream sounded like Mineta?"

At the sound of Mineta's name, Mina Ashido popped up in bed and said "Yechh" with the same level of disgust she reserved for her supplementary lessons with Aizawa.

"He got punished, right? I hope they really threw the book at him!" said Ashido, still good and angry about the night's earlier events.

"Seriously!" said Ochaco Uraraka from one corner of the room, where Tsuyu Asui was pressing on Uraraka's back to help her stretch.

"That boy will never learn until he actually gets hurt in the process, I fear," added Momo Yaoyorozu, who was busy organizing her things.

This was the space set aside for the girls of class A. It was a simple *washitsu* room with only six tatami mats, smaller than the boys' room since there were fewer girls to accommodate. There wasn't space for much else besides the girls' six futons, but since the room was only meant for sleeping anyway, it served its purpose. Raised in the lap of luxury, Yaoyorozu had at first been shocked and horrified by the cramped quarters, but she had quickly acclimated when the others explained that training camp was all about roughing it, so to speak.

"I should've stabbed his eye harder with my plug," grumbled Jiro.

"And I should've hit him with the acid that *really* burns!" said Ashido, thinking back to their triumph over Mineta when he'd attempted to peep at the class B girls.

Criminals and villains would always be persona non grata, but to these girls, those who committed sexually based offenses were especially heinous. While the rest of them were still fuming, Asui spoke up.

"I don't believe Mineta will ever truly change. He's been hurt plenty already, and it's never deterred him."

"You...may be right..." admitted Yaoyorozu.

They all reflected on the boy's past misdeeds and realized that if they were to represent Mineta as a pie chart, he would be a solid circle labeled "Lust." Asui's point was hard to deny.

"Even so, this particular offense was directed at the girls of another class... It's shameful that a fellow member of class A would do such a thing..." said Yaoyorozu with a somber shake of her head. As vice president, she felt a certain responsibility for keeping her cohort in line.

Suddenly, they heard a knock on the door and a voice.

"It's Kendo. Can we come in?"

UA

The girls of class A glanced at one another, unsure how to react to the unexpected visitors. Those lying in bed sat up, and after Yaoyorozu received small nods from each, she said "By all means" and opened the door. Itsuka Kendo led the pack. With her were Yui Kodai, Ibara Shiozaki, and Reiko Yanagi—a class B girl with bangs flopped over one eye. Kendo thrust a bag toward Yaoyorozu.

"As thanks, for earlier."

"Thanks for what?"

"Wait, what's going on?" said Ashido, intrigued by the bag and hoping to get a peek. She wasn't the only one—the other class A girls looked into the bag too, and Ashido yelped.

"Sweets!"

"Sorry, it's just kind of a mishmash of whatever we had on hand," explained Kendo, jostling the bag of individually packaged cookies, chocolates, and other goodies.

"To what do we owe this honor...?" asked

Yaoyorozu with a tilt of her head. "If you're referring to the incident with Mineta, think nothing of it! In fact, we should be apologizing to you for the appalling behavior of our classmate!"

She sounded like an abashed mother trying to make amends for a poorly raised, troublemaking son. At this, Kendo gave a puzzled smile.

"Don't sweat it. All's well that ends well, right?"

"Besides, we only caught him in the act because you girls warned us to start with," said Yanagi from behind Kendo. Beside her, Kodai muttered, "Mhm." Shiozaki took a step forward with hands clasped, as if in prayer.

"Please accept our gratitude and know that this is also on behalf of Tokage, Komori, and Tsunotori. They would have liked to thank you all in person too, but they were summoned by Vlad Sensei to review today's training session..."

Setsuna Tokage was a girl with sharp features who had nonetheless given class A a cheery shout-out back at the bus parking lot. Kinoko Komori was particularly petite, with a mushroom-shaped bob cut, and Pony Tsunotori was a charming girl with impressive horns and wide, round eyes.

"Exactly. It meant a lot to us, so here," said Kendo, thrusting the bag toward Yaoyorozu once more. The latter still had qualms about the gift, but Ashido jumped in and grabbed the bag with a "Thanks a lot!"

"Really now, Ashido..." started Yaoyorozu, but the others butted in.

"Come on, Momoyao. They got together to prepare this for us, so let's not be rude," said Jiro.

"Yes, Yaoyorozu. We can't just refuse the gift flat out," said Asui.

"But we only did what was natural..."

The generous gift still didn't sit well with Yaoyorozu, but this time Hagakure had an idea.

"How about we all eat this stuff together!"

Everyone turned to Hagakure's invisible face—presumably just above the collar of her floating pajama top—and could imagine a wide smile plastered across it.

"A slumber party! C'mon, since we're all here anyway!"

Slumber party. The words hung in the air for just a moment before smiles broke out all around.

"Yes! A chance like this doesn't come around too often."

"Sure… Slumber party…"

"Can we really?"

"Why the heck not? Pretty sure the boys are all hanging out together, too."

"Mhm."

"All agreed then?"

"Yeah, let's do it!"

U.A.

They sprang into action, spreading the sweets out in the middle of the room, buying a bunch of soft drinks from the nearby vending machine, and rolling up their futons to use in place of floor cushions. The girls of class A added their own snacks to the pile, and everyone raised cups for a toast. The sweets and good company put their bodies and minds at ease—this simple chance to chat and hang out was a welcome, exciting relief in the middle of training camp.

With slightly flushed cheeks, Yaoyorozu glanced around, unable to hold back her own delight.

"To tell the truth, this is my very first slumber party… Could someone explain how this is meant to go?"

"Well, you get a bunch of girls together, stuff your faces, and sit around chatting about whatever!" said Ashido. But Hagakure's invisible finger wagged in objection.

"Naw. Every good slumber party...demands talk about *amore*!"

The energy level in the room shot up a little.

"Yesss! The perfect slumber party topic!" agreed Ashido.

"Yikes, ha ha," said Uraraka, blushing.

"A conversation about love, then?" said Asui.

"Really...?" sighed Jiro.

"So that's where we're taking this, huh," said Kendo, forcing a smile.

"L-love? Before marriage, though?" gasped a flustered Yaoyorozu. The ever nunlike Shiozaki was on Yaoyorozu's side.

"I must agree. Marriage is a promise made before God..."

"A-more? A-more of a-what?" asked Yanagi, to which Kodai shook her head and said, "Nuh-uh."

Each girl was excited about this in her own way (or not), so the conversation switched to romance. Hagakure took charge and got the ball rolling.

"So, who's got a boyfriend?"

They all glanced around on obvious pins and needles, but nobody made a peep. The silence hung in the air for a moment before being broken by an aghast Hagakure.

"Huh? Nobody? Really?"

The energy subsided a little as the girls all shook their heads. None of them seemed to be hiding a secret relationship status, at any rate. A sense of gloom descended over the room.

They all had friends who'd gone on to normal high schools without hero programs, and those friends always had stories about so-and-so dating this one or that one. As these girls understood it, high school was supposed to be a time for reveling in young love.

"Well, not like there was time for that at the end of middle school, what with cramming for exams. And we haven't exactly had the luxury since starting U.A., either," said Kendo with a grimace, prompting profound nods from the group.

There was a lot to learn on the road to becoming pro heroes, so students of the Hero Course attended classes Monday through Saturday. Beyond the practical exercises, they also had ordinary school subjects with the usual homework and tests, so free time was a nearly foreign concept at this stage of their lives.

"Argh, but romance! I wanna hear something to tug at the heartstrings! How about crushes? Any of you gals crushing on someone?" said Ashido, leaning forward hungrily. The romance spark wouldn't be so easily snuffed out, and Ashido was more than willing to live it up vicariously if the others had stories to offer.

"Crushes, huh..." said Uraraka. She suddenly recalled Aoyama's words to her during the practical portion of their final exam, when he had suggested that she was crushing on Izuku Midoriya. The freckled face with green hair floated up into her mind's eye.

"Hmm? What's wrong, Ochaco?" asked Asui.

"Ah, I know that look!" said Hagakure, probably pointing at Uraraka's beet red face with an invisible finger. "There's def someone you're into!"

"N-no way. Sure isn't. Me? Naww."

"You're not helping your case, girl," said Hagakure.

"Who is it, who is it? We'll keep it a secret between us girls!" said Ashido.

As the two cupids closed in on Uraraka, her cheeks somehow grew even redder than usual. She panicked.

"Nah, y'see, my thing, it's not like that."

"Your *thing*, huh? What thing is that?"

"Just spit it out already. You're totally in love with someone, right?"

"Seriously, not like that!"

Hagakure and Ashido were coming after her like a pair of hard-boiled detectives, and at the word *love*, Midoriya's face popped into her head again. She waved her hands around to chase away the image and accidentally grazed her interrogators, sending them floating into the air with her "Zero Gravity" Quirk.

"Huhh?"

"Ahh!"

"Oops, sorry!" said Uraraka, bringing her fingertips together and canceling the effects. The two girls flopped down onto some futons.

"Like I said, that's not it! It's just been a while since

I got together with girls to chat about junk like this, so it got my blood pumping, I guess?"

"Been a while? That's all, huh," said Jiro, clearly exasperated. Hagakure and Ashido apologized and adjusted themselves back into position. Uraraka was still feeling awkward, but she breathed a small sigh and stroked her chest, relieved at having fooled the others.

Hmm? Fooled them? Nah, I just got them off my back, right? After all, what do I have to hide? I only started thinking about it cuz Aoyama had to go and be all weird... Thinking about it? Nah, not even that far. And thinking about what, exactly? Me and Deku? It's not like that... Not us! We're not together or anything. Just, like, connected or whatever. No biggie.

Uraraka's mind raced, sending her tumbling backward onto her futon.

"Everything okay, Ochaco? You suddenly look exhausted," asked Asui.

"Just trying to stop my heart from pounding, heh..."

"Do you need a doctor? That could be a sign of something worse."

"I wish a doctor could cure what I've got…"

"How awful, that the body would react in such a way to the topic of love… Could the Lord truly have been so cruel while creating us?" said Shiozaki, gently stroking Uraraka's head with all the compassion she could muster. This only got Ashido fired up again.

"See? This is why us girls gotta open up about romance every so often! So let's hear it—any actual crushes?"

Nobody so much as twitched this time.

"We could always talk about literally anything else," suggested Yanagi.

"Ugh, but my heartstrings are still begging for some tugging! I can't help being a girlie girl."

It wasn't that Ashido wanted a boyfriend of her own, really. She wasn't after love for herself, since she knew full well that she and the others had to devote themselves to their hero education for the time being. That said, once the seed of romance was planted in her brain, it had to sprout and bloom. She needed that tight-chested feeling that only came from the perfect sappy story. That sweet shudder down the spine, sparked by schmaltz. The almost-magical

sensation that filled the heart to bursting. That could sustain Ashido in the meantime, feeding the girlie girl within, and what better time to refuel than these precious few evening hours of training camp? This jumble of emotions reached the other girls wordlessly, but though they nodded at her, not one of them could come up with a romantic anecdote of her own.

UA

The conversation had come to a standstill again, but Hagakure had another idea.

"How about we get our fill with, uh, y'know, hypotheticals!"

"How, exactly?" asked Asui. Yanagi looked just as wary and said, "That might not end well."

"What I'm trying to say is...use our imaginations! Fantasize! Like, is there any boy in class A or B you'd wanna date? That kinda thing."

"That could work," said Ashido, fully on board.

"Choosing a single boy, though, I don't know..." said Yaoyorozu.

"Slumber parties are all about easy, breezy chatting, though. Just another way for us to communicate about anything we want," offered Kendo as if she was an old hand at this, smiling and sitting cross-legged on the other side of the circle from Yaoyorozu. The latter was immediately impressed by the former's open-minded attitude.

"I suppose so... Every experience can be a valuable lesson, somehow."

"C'mon, then... Who would you guys wanna date?"

"Picking a boyfriend, huh..."

The girls fell into deep thought. So deep that they didn't notice Uraraka blushing and shaking her head again.

"None of them really spring to mind as boyfriend material," said Ashido, pouting, as if she'd gone out for a shopping spree only to be disappointed by the items on sale.

"True. Never really looked at any of them that way," said Kendo.

"I view them as classmates, fellow heroes in training, and rivals, even..." confessed Yaoyorozu.

"Isn't it more telling that we don't even see these

guys as potential boyfriends?" said Jiro.

"That sounds like a quick way to end this conversation," said Asui.

Yaoyorozu gasped, remembering something.

"Hmm? Gonna tell us who you wanna go out with, Momoyao?" asked Ashido. She drew close to Yaoyorozu in hot anticipation, but Yaoyorozu responded with an awkward smile.

"No, not me. I was thinking of Jiro."

"Huh? What about me?"

Jiro was caught off guard, and Yaoyorozu blushed a little as she tried her hand at romance talk.

"I was just recalling how well you seem to get along with Kaminari... What do you say to that?"

"Ugh, knock it off! He's just easy to talk to, is all. But totally the type of flake to cheat on a girl, first chance he got."

Jiro's face scrunched in clear embarrassment, and to her left, Asui put one finger to her lower lip.

"You really think so? I actually believe Kaminari would make for a loyal boyfriend."

"Do tell, Asui. Does that mean Kaminari is your type?"

"No. Not in the least. But as a rule, he's always a gentleman when it comes to girls."

"Only cuz he's a big fat womanizer," said Jiro in a bashful huff.

At the word *womanizer*, the exact same image popped into every girl's mind, and practically in sync, they muttered some version of "Anyone's better than Mineta."

"Mhm," said Kodai, late to join the chorus. The girls burst out laughing, suddenly feeling united in their struggle against the one villain they had in common.

"I'd take anyone in the whole world over Mineta!" Ashido said to Kendo, wiping tears from her eyes. "Anyone in class B similar to him?"

"No way. Our boys are pretty straight arrows, actually. Buncha hard-liners. Ah, we've got Monoma, of course," replied Kendo with a dismissive wave of her hand. Neito Monoma harbored a competitive spirit against class A, sometimes to an unsettling extent.

"Monoma, he's just..." started Yanagi.

"Mhm," added Kodai.

"How do I put this..."

"Mhm."

The girls of class B were accepting of their some-what eccentric classmate, despite his faults.

"He's actually not bad looking, so it's a shame he's such a wacko!" said Hagakure, holding nothing back.

"Speaking of hot dudes, how about Todoroki?" said Ashido. Everyone pictured Shoto Todoroki and couldn't help but agree. The handsome boy was the independent sort who lived life at his own pace, and the girls couldn't think of a single downside to Todoroki until Kendo spoke up.

"Oh, you mean Endeavor's kid?"

The thought of Todoroki's fiery father stopped them in their tracks. No way a relationship would survive with the number two hero breathing down your necks.

"Yep, I'm thinking nope."

"The guy'd probably be a real jerk to any girl dating his son..."

The girls of class A shrank at the thought of the imposing Endeavor, while Shiozaki alone was moved by compassion.

"Those with the fiercest temperaments often have the deepest wounds. If only someone could pluck the thorn from that man's soul..."

"You wanna get with *Endeavor*, Ibara?" gasped

Kendo. The father of a schoolmate? Romance with a pro hero? Unthinkable. But Shiozaki maintained her composure and shook her head.

"All creatures great and small are deserving of love. No, I only speak of healing, not lust. Besides, the man is hardly my type..."

"Don't spook us like that," said Yanagi flatly.

"Mhm," said Kodai with a nod.

Uraraka rubbed her chest and spoke up.

"You sure are a serious one, Shiozaki!"

"Serious? Nobody's as serious as Ida," said Asui.

"Oh, your class president, right?"

"You can tell that dear Ida would never cheat on a girlfriend. Why, he'd probably be his usual serious self, even on dates..." said Yaoyorozu. Everyone suddenly imagined it—the boy would turn a date into a stiff, formal affair. And after that, who could say?

"How many years would it take before Ida'd be willing to hold hands, y'think?"

"He'd probably wanna get married, first..."

"Har, har. Good one, girls," laughed Kendo. They shook their heads at her, though.

"No, it's entirely possible, given how Ida is," said Asui.

"You mean it?"

"The guy is beyond serious about ev-er-y-thing."

The girls realized how exhausting that particular relationship would be, and Ida was quickly eliminated as a viable option.

"How about Midoriya?" said Ashido. Hearing that name, Uraraka's heart started to pound again. It was getting a workout, this night.

"I swear, I don't get that kid," admitted Kendo.

"Midoriya? How so?"

"Take the Sports Festival, for instance. He dug up all those land mines during the race, right? Totally insane strategy, but bold as hell. And then in the tournament, he's an all-out, bare-knuckle brawler. But when I spot him in the hall or cafeteria, he gives off a totally different vibe."

Uraraka opened her mouth to respond, but the swirling jumble of emotions kept her from forming words, so all that emerged was a "Hmm." Asui spoke up instead.

"Midoriya, right... He's just about the hardest worker you'll ever meet. It's like everything he does is aimed at getting him one step closer to being a hero."

Asui looked around for confirmation of her interpretation. Uraraka came to her support with a weighty nod and finally found the words.

"Seeing Deku in action just makes me wanna do my best too!"

Witnessing Uraraka do her darndest to get across that exact feeling, Kendo grinned at her.

"Yeah, I get it. It's great when someone can inspire others like that."

Uraraka smiled back, happy to know that, just maybe, Kendo understood what made Midoriya special.

"Oh, but he's kinda, like, an insane All Might fanboy," added Ashido.

"He'd probably cancel on a date if there was an All Might meet and greet to go to instead!" said Hagakure.

"Yes. I do believe he would do that," agreed Yaoyorozu.

"Huh? Even though we see the guy at school all the time?" asked Yanagi, referring to All Might's recent decision to become a teacher at U.A.

"That's Midoriya for ya," said Ashido with a heavy nod.

"Or he'd ask his girlfriend to come along to meet All

Might," suggested Hagakure.

"You're...not wrong, there."

Uraraka could easily imagine such a date with the boy.

"Not boyfriend material, then," said Yanagi flatly, thereby eliminating Midoriya.

"Nuh-uh," added Kodai.

Uraraka was relieved to be moving on from Midoriya. Still, something about it bugged her, and she made a sour face.

"How about Bakugo?" she suggested.

"No way," said Jiro, instantly ending Bakugo's chances. "He's smart and he's probably got a bright future, but...that personality. Yeeeesh."

The girls discussed the rest of the boys in succession, but each got eliminated by one harsh judgment or another, like so many soap bubbles popping into nothing. The very last one bit the dust, still with no heartstring tugs to speak of.

"Ugh... Don't tell me I'm gonna have to go off to my extra lessons without a single bit of lovey-dovey goodness to keep me going?" groaned Ashido.

UA

Ashido slumped over in despair, like a weary desert traveler in desperate need of water. Hagakure, hoping to come to her aid, thought for a moment.

"Maybe we've been going at it, like, backward? I mean, if we were boys and the boys were girls, which of them would make good girlfriends?" she said with what was most likely a wide grin.

"A change in perspective, huh?" mused Ashido.

They tried to picture their male classmates turning into girls, which in most cases just meant imagining those same muscular boys with long hair.

"Yeah, not doing it for me…"

"Us, choosing girl versions of them? My heartstrings aren't feeling anything over here…"

"No, it could work!" insisted Hagakure with a giggle. Nearby, Yanagi stared at Kendo.

"You'd have tons of luck with the ladies as a boy, Itsuka."

"Me? Y'think?" asked Kendo, wide-eyed. Yanagi nodded and said, "You're the coolest one of us, in class B." Kodai added a "Mhmm" in support.

"Quite true. A single word from you, Kendo, is enough to shepherd our wayward classmates. You're evenhanded. Strict, yet warm... And eminently capable," said Shiozaki.

Yaoyorozu was inspired to add her own praise. "During our internship, you helped carry me along when I was feeling like deadweight. Without you, I fear I might have grown despondent, even."

Both Yaoyorozu and Kendo had interned with Snake Hero: Uwabami, but the commercial shoot they'd endured had made Yaoyorozu question the very nature of hero work.

"Naw, we both backed each other up. And cut it out, guys. I'm blushing over here," said Kendo, slightly uncomfortable with all the attention.

"Plus, we already know you stick up for women, since you knocked Mineta for a loop earlier," said Asui.

"That was awesome!" shouted Uraraka.

This got Ashido thinking. "I bet you'd slap the living daylights outta pervs and gropers! As a boy-friend, you'd probably be all like, 'Hands off my chick, punk!'"

The whole group practically squealed, now imagining male Kendo defending their honor and driving off would-be harassers. Yes, Kendo would make the ideal boyfriend—sympathetic to girls' feelings and ready to protect them at a moment's notice.

"Hang on, now we're getting lovey-dovey over a girl!" said Ashido, coming to her senses.

"Hey, don't blame me," said Kendo with a grin. "Maybe the love angle just isn't gonna work. How about thinking of it from the sidekick perspective? Like, working alongside a boy?"

"Sidekicks, huh…" said Ashido.

"Or wait, no. What if you could be one of the boys for a day?"

The girls thought about Kendo's suggestion, and one particular boy popped into Uraraka's mind.

"I'd wanna be Bakugo for a day."

"Eh? Him, really?" asked a shocked Jiro. Uraraka smiled and blushed.

"Mhm. He gave me a solid beating at the Sports Festival, right? During that battle, I really got a feel for how strong he is. Might be awesome to get a taste of that strength, myself!"

"Bakugo is quite strong, yes. With a keen sense for battle," remarked Yaoyorozu.

"Exactly! If I got to be Bakugo, I'd wanna get in a fight and just go nuts!" said Uraraka, throwing a few snappy punches.

"I hear ya..." said Ashido. "In that case, I'd choose Sero. Always wanted to try shooting that tape of his! Since I get bored of my acid sometimes. How about you, Momoyao?"

"If I had to pick? Koda. The notion of controlling animals fascinates me."

"Mhm," said Kodai, who would've also picked Koji Koda.

Jiro worked up the courage to make her choice.

"Kaminari, I guess? I'd wanna fire off some electricity and feel what it's really like when he goes into dummy mode. Just once! Once would be enough for a lifetime."

"I would choose...Tokoyami," said Asui. "Fighting alongside Dark Shadow and having it live inside you? I have to wonder what that's like."

"I'll take Sato!" said Hagakure. "Eating all those sweets and turning them into power? No extra chub, so no guilt!"

"Girl, you're invisible. Not like we could tell if you put on weight anyway," pointed out Ashido.

"Sure you could! My clothes would reveal the curves."

Kendo listened to the other girls chatter, somewhat shocked. She sighed and smiled.

"Not so hard to choose once we're off the topic of love, huh?"

And it was true. Where the lovey-dovey talk had sputtered, the conversation about trying out other Quirks got their imaginations going.

"Gahh! We didn't get anywhere with the romance stuff!" said Ashido, flopping back in defeat. The other girls exchanged pained smiles.

"Good luck with your extra lessons, heh," said Jiro.

"Surely our failure here was a sign from God," said Shiozaki.

"Nooo!" cried Ashido, flailing atop her futon in defiance of the naysayers.

"Still..." said Asui, "They say you 'fall' in love, right? It's not something you can help, and when it happens, you'd probably want to tell someone about

those feelings. We can always revisit the romance talk if and when that day comes."

The thought of real love, someday. A distant possibility. Would they be heroes by then, with the pride and confidence to pursue romance? With eyes toward the future, the girls grinned, their smiles full of love.

LA

The warm and fuzzy moment didn't last long for Ashido, who was dreading the supplementary lessons with Aizawa.

"I need my fix, though! Anything! The tiniest romantic convo!"

Forget the distant future—she wanted it now. A dose of inspiration to help her survive summer school hell.

"Gotta come up with something quick, then... Ah, how about, like, what *type* of guys we're into?"

"Yeah! What's your type, Mina?"

"Well... He's gotta be strong! But also with a childish side sometimes? A wild guy who plays by his own rules but always sticks by your side!"

Strong, childish, always by one's side… The girls of class A listened intently and all came up with the same thought.

"That sounds just like Dark Shadow," said Asui.

"Totally true!"

They leaped to agree with Asui before Ashido could get a word in edgewise.

"Dark Shadow? That's Tokoyami's Quirk, like you mentioned earlier, right?" asked a bewildered Kendo.

"Yeah! But…" pouted Ashido. "It's not a person!"

"It's so strong, though," said Asui. "Today, just before lunch, I peeked into the cave where Tokoyami was training. Dark Shadow was unbelievably fierce in that darkness. Really giving Tokoyami a hard time."

"And then, when it's light out, it gets all cute! Always going 'Yup!' and 'Yep!'" said Uraraka, thinking back to Dark Shadow's more charming moments.

"During our final exam, I was teamed up with Tokoyami. He mentioned how Ectoplasm Sensei's Quirk was particularly powerful, and Dark Shadow whined, 'I'm powerful too,'" added Asui.

"Wow. That is cute, actually," said Yanagi.

"Mhm," agreed Kodai.

Even these two seemed to relax their typically stern expressions.

Hagakure added, "So it's childish too!"

"This Dark Shadow doesn't sound half bad," said Kendo in earnest. The other girls nodded, as if Dark Shadow were a transfer student they hadn't remembered up to this point.

"You guys can't be serious..." grumbled Ashido.

"Plus, it's a Quirk, so it's always by your side," said Jiro.

"Always by Tokoyami's side, more like!" shouted Ashido.

"Guess that makes Tokoyami your type, since Dark Shadow totally makes him the complete package!" teased Hagakure.

"That's not how any of this works!" said Ashido, practically snorting in frustration. "I'm getting my heartstrings tugged tonight if it kills me! Next up is... which pro hero would you wanna marry?"

The girls flinched at the question but were soon laughing it up once again.

Gossip, compliments, judgments, pure delight—this roundtable had it all. And while the romance talk may have stalled, the girls were feeling warm, fuzzy, and fulfilled before long. The slumber party was far from over.

Part 5
Over the Top

"Coming in!"

The boys of class A turned to see the sliding screen of their large room smack open, as if a rival gang had come to throw down.

"Well, look who it is," said Eijiro Kirishima with a grin, as the class B boys stepped into the room, fresh from their session in the rotenburo. Only a small table separated the two factions. Tetsutetsu Tetsutetsu led class B forward and roared, "We've kept you waiting, but this is going down *now*!"

Nobody was here to make friends. The smiles on these boys' faces were aggressive. Competitive. Some didn't relish the thought of battle, though not one among them could be called timid or weakhearted.

Because everyone in that room knew that classes A and B were fated to clash.

Men are thought to be creatures that instinctively seek out battle, so a gathering of men such as this could end only one way. A fight without reason or conviction would be mindless violence—but these boys certainly had a reason.

It had begun a few hours earlier.

A day of brutal Quirk training had pushed the U.A. Hero Course students to the breaking point, and then some. When a body is forced to go beyond its natural limits, it instinctively seeks rest and nourishment. The nutrients and comfort promised by their dinner represented the light at the end of this gauntlet of a tunnel, so at the massive wooden tables just in front of the lodge, the students practically inhaled the Japanese-style curry they'd cooked for themselves.

"Tomorrow night, we're having *nikujaga* stew," declared Mandalay.

Meat, potatoes, and vegetables, stewed in a soy sauce base with a bit of sugar—the dish was a staple of Japanese comfort food. Even with bellies already full of curry, the boys in particular couldn't help but get excited for the next day's nikujaga dinner. Mandalay went on.

"We've got both beef and pork available, so you kids decide which class gets which."

This stirred the pot.

"Nikujaga's obviously gotta have pork, right?"

"Um, no. Beef."

Pork was traditional in eastern Japan, while the western parts of the country favored beef. Even then, it could vary from household to household, regardless of region. Seeing this sudden split of opinion, Tenya Ida stood up and begun to flap his hands wildly.

"We had better make up our minds! Wouldn't you agree, Kendo?"

"Sure thing. How about a round of rock-paper-scissors? Winning side gets first pick?" suggested Itsuka Kendo, standing to meet Ida's challenge.

"No objections? In that case..."

"Now, now, wait a minute!" said Neito Monoma of

class B, just as the two class presidents were about to throw hands. "A silly game? To decide something so important? No fun. Why not a more worthy battle?"

"What's wrong with rock-paper-scissors?" asked Kendo.

Monoma snorted. "I expected more from you, Kendo. This is a rare chance to go head-to-head with our mortal enemies in class A. What a waste, to do so with a trifling match of rock-paper-scissors."

"Like I'm always saying, there're no 'mortal enemies' here."

All eyes were now on Monoma, with all thoughts on his absurd grudge against class A.

"Pork? Beef? Does anyone actually care?" asked Reiko Yanagi.

"Mhm, mhm," said Yui Kodai, nodding in support. Tetsutetsu also came in swinging with passionate indifference.

"Long as we're tearing into meat, any kind's all right by me!"

The other boys agreed, especially Kirishima, whose friendship with Tetsutetsu had grown ever since they'd fought at the Sports Festival.

"Every sorta meat's a winner in my book! They're all tasty!"

"So true, man," shot back Tetsutetsu. The two boys grinned and flashed each other thumbs-ups.

They shared more than just a love for meat, since Kirishima's "Hardening" Quirk and Tetsutetsu's "Steel" produced remarkably similar effects. As it happened, both were also hot-blooded hard-liners who valued a certain brand of chivalry above all else. Their solidarity began to convince everyone else that meat was meat was meat, but Monoma wasn't having it.

"Hmm? All tasty? Perhaps, but true nikujaga must feature pork. Everyone knows that," he said, though in truth he couldn't have cared less. Monoma had a compulsion for fanning the flames of competition in the hopes of beating class A at something—anything. And he knew exactly which of class A's fuses to light.

"Ah, but if class A really doesn't care either way, then we can skip this little showdown and just have our class choose. I can't abide by beef in my nikujaga, so class B will get pork, okay? Does that sound fair, *Bakugo*?"

"Huhh?"

Monoma was sure to cast a lip-curling sneer in Bakugo's direction, reminding the latter of the time their teams had clashed during the Sports Festival's cavalry battle. Bakugo's beastly hunger for victory and bold tactics had triumphed over Monoma's strategy, but unlike with Kirishima and Tetsutetsu, the encounter hadn't led to a healthy, friendly rivalry. It wasn't exactly a grudge, but these two were hardly fans of each other.

"You're fine with beef, right, Bakugo? I'm sure you wanted that delicious pork real badly, but your class A chums decided to throw in the towel, so you'll just have to watch class B enjoy our pork nikujaga tomorrow." A clear taunt from Monoma.

"Like hell I will. I want freaking pork!" roared Bakugo. He didn't actually care about the choice of meat either, but the bundle of conceit known as Bakugo couldn't stand by while class B's instigator threw his weight around.

"Then I suppose we'll need to compete to decide," said Monoma casually.

"Damn right! I'll destroy you class B goons if it means we get to have pork!"

The boys of class B flinched.

"Who the hell're you calling 'goons'?" yelled Tetsutetsu.

"You, for starters!" shot back Bakugo.

"Sorry, Tetsutetsu! Bakugo just can't help himself when it comes to name-calling," said Kirishima.

"That's goon talk if ever I heard it, broomhead!" said Bakugo, turning on his own classmate.

At Bakugo's declaration of war, Ida shot up in protest, waving his arms up and down.

"Bakugo! You must stop speaking for all of us... Especially during our all-important training camp! This is not meant to be a competition!"

"Think I care? This fool brought the fight, so I ain't backing down!"

"You're the one picking a fight now," said Juzo Honenuki, the skull-faced boy sitting next to Tetsutetsu. Monoma had lit Bakugo's fuse, and now Bakugo's bad attitude was riling up the other boys of class B.

"Sensei!" cried Momo Yaoyorozu, looking to Aizawa to intercede, but the teacher only stood back and observed.

"Let them."

"But...?"

"Outside of training, what you kids do you with your time is your choice. As long as you don't cause trouble for the lodge," said Aizawa, causing Ida to gasp in understanding.

"Aha, but of course! Our free time is our own... and with that independence comes the opportunity to engage in friendly rivalry, which will in turn make us better fighters and heroes someday... How brilliant, Sensei!"

"Sure, I guess."

Blind to his teacher's annoyance and apathy, Ida had managed to convince himself of a point that nobody was trying to make.

"Why don't we settle this with arm wrestling, everyone?" proposed the straitlaced class president.

UA

And so the boys would fight for the right to meat, perhaps as a throwback to ancient times, when men

stalked the mighty mammoth across the frozen plains. Unlike cavewomen waiting for their menfolk to return from a successful hunt, though, the girls of classes A and B were already deep into their slumber party when the B boys stormed the A room. Incidentally, the boys hadn't noticed Minoru Mineta's conspicuous absence. Not when they were about to stake their pride on a battle for meat—a battle to be decided on a small table in the center of the room.

"You actually showed up, you copycat bastard," said Bakugo, sneering at Monoma.

"Thought I would run from a chance to crush class A once and for all? Never," said Monoma. His ploy to rile up Bakugo had gone exactly according to plan, and Monoma now shot a provocative grin back at class A's powder keg.

"Mark my words, class B will feast upon pork tomorrow! I can picture it now—the jealous look on your faces. Like so many whimpering dogs!" continued Monoma, ending with a maniacal laugh befitting a villain.

"Not after I pound you into the dirt! That pork's gonna be all mine!"

"Hang on!" said Hanta Sero. "You don't get to hog the pork!"

"*Sigh*… This is all getting kinda ridiculous," said Izuku Midoriya.

"Sure is," said Shoto Todoroki. Neither cared about the matter of the meat, but with both groups of boys fired up, these two couldn't very well sit it out.

Ida stood up between the two teams. His serious nature made him the ideal referee—a point that both classes had agreed upon earlier, by majority rule. Monoma had been the only voice of dissent, suggesting that Ida might sneakily favor his own class.

"It's time to begin the arm wrestling," said Ida, signaling for the chosen competitors from each class to step forward. Two teams of five, pure tests of strength, no Quirks allowed. Winning three or more matches would grant overall victory.

From class A, Mashirao Ojiro, Mezo Shoji, Koji Koda, Eijiro Kirishima, and Katsuki Bakugo.

Representing class B, Nirengeki Shoda, Juzo Honenuki, Jurota Shishida, Yosetsu Awase, and Tetsutetsu Tetsutetsu.

It seemed that both classes' lineups were prioritizing

power and grip strength. Bakugo scanned the rival squad before glaring at a rather nonchalant-looking Monoma.

"All that talk, talk, talk, and you ain't even gonna fight?" said Bakugo.

"Do I look like a muscled brute to you? No. I will play the role of strategist," explained Monoma.

Midoriya murmured, "Incredible," impressed by anyone bold enough to provoke Bakugo and then continue to shove it in his face, like a bullfighter waving a cape. Meanwhile, Todoroki—though watching attentively from the sidelines—was overcome by postdinner drowsiness and couldn't stifle a big yawn.

"Tch. Let's just get this over with!" said Bakugo, mostly to Ida. But the latter tilted his head and said, "I feel as though we're forgetting something…" He glanced at the clock on the wall. "Of course! It's nearly time for the supplemental lessons!"

Kirishima, Sero, Denki Kaminari, and Rikido Sato groaned audibly. The change to the bathing schedule had also moved up their lesson time.

"Ugh, but I don't wanna!" whined Kaminari, like he'd been sentenced to a temporary trip to hell.

"No choice, Kaminari. Let's get this over with," said Sero, dragging his reluctant friend.

"Might as well give it our all!" added Sato, striking a powerful pose as the trio left the room.

The problem was Kirishima. He was a key member of the arm wrestling team, but the extra lessons had completely slipped his mind.

"I'll just, uh, find a chance to sneak back here and compete!" said Kirishima.

"Kirishima! Your supplemental lessons are not to be shirked!"

"I'll just say I gotta take a whiz at some point! Should be fine!"

But there was little pep in Kirishima's step as he slunk out of the room, and the loss of one of team A's brawlers was palpable. Monoma didn't miss this chance.

"What's this, now? The mighty class A had some failures after all? And your team's lost a member? You might as well surrender now and be done with it!" he said with another shrill laugh. The worst part? Every word was true, so the boys of class A were stunned into silence.

"On that note, I'd better be off to my own extra lessons," said Monoma, turning toward the door.

"You too?"

"I'll find an opportunity to slip out as well. Worry not."

"Monoma is really impressive..." murmured Midoriya, unable to hide the respect in his voice.

"Or just a loser," said Todoroki, fighting back another yawn.

"Anyhow, let us begin!" said Ida loud and clear, attempting to shoo away the strange mood brought on by Monoma's departure. "The first match is Ojiro versus Shoda!" Shoda, from class B, was short and somewhat plump, while Ojiro's narrow eyes made him stand out in a plain way. The two boys stepped up to either side of the table and kneeled.

"Here's to a good match, Ojiro."

"You bet."

These two had history. During the cavalry battle a few months back, both had been brainwashed into helping Hitoshi Shinso, a boy from General Studies. Shinso's team had placed high, but Ojiro and Shoda hadn't felt comfortable advancing to the tournament

when they had no memory of the previous event. Instead, they'd stuck to their convictions and withdrawn with zero regrets.

Now their hands met atop the table, Shoda's chubby, baby-like hand contrasting with Ojiro's solid, muscular one.

"Are you both ready?" asked Ida, placing one hand over theirs and checking that their elbows were resting on the table properly. Simple arm wrestling or not, an intense aura of competition had filled the large room. The class A boys had high hopes for Ojiro. His Quirk gave him a long, sturdy tail, but his real weapon, so to speak, was his propensity for martial arts. He was a born fighter.

"Ready...go!" shouted Ida, and it was over in an instant.

"Great going, Nirengeki!"

Shoda had annihilated Ojiro, leaving the latter dumbstruck and the former with a proud, almost bashful smile.

"The hell? What was that crap, Tail Guy?" said Bakugo, fuming.

"To think that Ojiro would be slain..." said Fumikage Tokoyami, hardly able to believe his eyes.

"Sorry, guys. He got me before I could even react…" gasped Ojiro, still stunned.

Midoriya, however, had been watching closely. His motormouth began analyzing.

"Interesting. Shoda was definitely faster, but his little hands didn't hint at that at all… Ojiro couldn't imagine getting taken down by a baby hand… In fact, he might've even been scared of hurting his opponent. So the small, soft hands were really a trap, and the strategy worked like a charm. Could even be used against villains, to throw them off guard? Give them a weak handshake, and then BAM? Shoda's whole look is nonthreatening, actually. If he can exploit that and catch opponents while their defenses are down, he can do that much more damage."

Midoriya's dedication to becoming a hero frequently led him to hypothesize how one strategy or another could be used against villains. Shoda overheard the boy's frantic muttering, though, and looked troubled.

"Nope, actually. I just arm wrestled like normal."

"Ugh, shut the hell up! Next match!" said Bakugo, not giving class B time to revel in its victory.

"Will you ever learn to restrain that mouth of

yours?" replied Ida, before calling Shoji and Honenuki to the table.

"Good luck, Shoji!" said Midoriya.

"Victory here will bring untold pride..." said Tokoyami, supporting his classmate.

"If you win, I will happily lend you my laser pointer, ☆" said Aoyama, but the reply from a mouth on the end of one of Shoji's dupli-arms was simply, "No thanks."

It was only natural that class B's early win had fired up class A.

"Ready...go!"

Muscle clashed with muscle, and both arms shook violently. Inspired by their previous win, class B gave a rousing cheer, but to no avail. The balance quickly shifted, and Shoji's bulky arm brought Honenuki's crashing down onto the table.

"Wow. Not bad," said Todoroki, sounding almost impressed. Class A cheered, class B groaned, and Bakugo gave a haughty "Hmph!" that could not go ignored by Tetsutetsu.

"Who died and made him king of the world?" said class B's firebrand.

Now class B was eager to get to the third match. Representing class A was Koda, a shy boy with a stony-looking body, while class B sent out Shishida, whose glasses seemed at odds with his otherwise beastly appearance. Judging by looks alone, this match was anyone's guess.

"Get it done, Koda!"

"Take 'im down, Jurota!"

With cheers coming from both sides, Koda and Shishida clasped hands.

"Ready...go!"

There was little motion. They were evenly matched. Shishida roared, determined not to give an inch, while Koda endured with all his might.

"C'mon, Koda!"

"Don't give up, Jurota!"

Koda slowly began to exhaust Shishida's impressive stamina, but while the rest of the boys whooped in the hopes of breaking the stalemate, nobody noticed who had just snuck back into the room.

"Go, do it!"

"Don't fold, Jurota!"

Amid the screams and cries, one voice suddenly stuck out like a sore thumb.

"Ack, a bug!"

"Eeek?" yelped Koda, who feared bugs and couldn't help but flinch. Shishida felt the pressure against his arm slacken and made his move, pinning Koda's hand under his own.

"What...? Ugh, Monoma? When'd you creep back in here?"

"Just now, in fact."

As promised, Monoma had slipped out of his lessons just in time to shift the tides of match three. Meanwhile, Koda was now cowering behind Ida, frantically scanning for stray bugs.

"Calm yourself, Koda! I don't see any insects about."

"Ohh? I could have sworn I spotted a bug. Perhaps I was wrong," said Monoma.

"You won't be interfering again once I'm done with you!" said Bakugo, practically leaping at Monoma, but the latter maintained his devil-may-care attitude.

"That's quite the accusation, considering you have no proof. Blaming me for your team's loss? Now that's just sour grapes! Awful! Terrible! Anyhow, I'd best be getting back."

"Huhh? I swear, I'll..." cursed Bakugo under his breath as Monoma flitted out of the room.

"Monoma's not really a bad guy... He just cares a little too much about class B and our pride..." said Shoda apologetically.

"Tell it to someone who cares! Hey, Rocky! You're seriously scared of freaking bugs?"

Koda seemed to deflate as Bakugo tore into him, but Tokoyami tried to comfort his friend.

"We all have our demons... Don't let it get to you."

The score was now two to one, in class B's favor, and a third win would mean total victory.

"Match four is Kirishima versus Awase, but..." began Ida.

"What now?" asked Awase, the bandanna-wearing boy who'd stepped up to the table.

"Hrm..." pondered Ida. "Kirishima said he would attempt to make it back for a moment, but he clearly hasn't found a chance. Shall we have Bakugo face Tetsutetsu now? Or choose a replacement for Kirishima?"

"I'll take my turn, sure thing!" said Tetsutetsu, making the decision easy for the troubled referee.

Bakugo had other thoughts.

"Hell no. The title match has gotta come last."

"Huh? Why's it always gotta be about you, any-how?" said Tetsutetsu, not backing down.

"Give it a rest, metalhead."

As he watched the confrontation, Midoriya found Tetsutetsu's boldness particularly refreshing. And Bakugo had barely changed at all. A funny expression arose on Midoriya's face.

Scary how used to this I am...

Tetsutetsu and Bakugo's war of words was about to escalate when Kirishima burst into the room.

"Sorry I'm late!" said Kirishima.

"Just on time actually, Kirishima!" said Ida.

"Phew. What's the score?"

"Two to one, and we're losing."

"Yikes! Well, I'd better bring my A game!"

Kirishima and Awase locked hands, and Tetsutetsu and Bakugo put their squabble aside to watch.

"Ready...go!"

Awase took an early lead, swiftly bringing the back of Kirishima's hand several hairbreadths from the table. Kirishima endured, but the awkward angle put him at a huge disadvantage.

"You're not done yet, Kirishima!"

"Go, go, Awase!"

The cheers got louder and louder, and things looked dire for Kirishima until a roar from Bakugo shook the room.

"Kirishima! Lose this thing and you're *dead*!"

The absurd threat caught everyone off guard, including Awase, giving Kirishima the chance he needed to swing his arm up and over the top. Awase's hand hit the table with a smack.

"Thanks for being so supportive, dude!" said Kirishima with a smile, leaving everyone wondering how a threat on his life from Bakugo qualified as support.

In any case, the score was tied, which meant the title match would decide it all. Bakugo and Tetsutetsu stomped toward the table, finally ready to show what they were made of.

"Bakugo…or Tetsutetsu…? Argh, who'm I s'posed to root for?" said Kirishima, clutching his head. Tetsutetsu could sense Kirishima's struggle to choose

one friend or the other, so he flashed the latter a thumbs-up.

"Kirishima! Don't worry about me, bro!"

"Sorry, Tetsutetsu! But I'm in class A! You get it, right, man?"

"Shut. Up!" said Bakugo, interrupting the melodramatic macho moment.

"Bring it home for us, Bakugo!" said Kirishima.

The boys placed their elbows on the table, locked hands, and glared at each other.

"At the word *go*, you're dead meat."

"Naww, class B's taking home the prize today!"

"Gentlemen, the match hasn't started yet! Release each other!" said Ida.

They'd jumped the gun and started the battle on pure instinct, but the referee forced them to back off and reset. Bakugo and Tetsutetsu breathed deeply and awaited the starting signal.

UA

"Ready...go!"

Bakugo was quicker on the draw. In a repeat of

what had happened to Kirishima in the previous match, Tetsutetsu's hand suddenly hovered just above the surface of the table, but he fought back and started lifting Bakugo's arm. The grin Bakugo shot him almost seemed to applaud his efforts. Each poured all his strength into his arm, pushing back against the other with waves of force. Power against power, the bones and muscles of their arms practically creaked under the pressure. It was a breathless, evenly matched back-and-forth.

"Go, Bakugo!"

"End this game, Tetsutetsu!"

The audience was just as fired up as the competitors now. Unimaginably so, considering that the stakes were the rights to a bit of pork. As the seconds passed, though, the gap in raw talent became apparent. Bakugo began to read his opponent's breathing, and Tetsutetsu's wrist started to crumple backward. With the balance broken, Bakugo's arm advanced mercilessly, slowly grinding down Tetsutetsu's.

"Tetsutetsu!"

"Bakugo!"

The voices from class B had notes of horror and despair, while those of class A echoed with glee.

"Don't you lose, Tetsutetsu!" screamed Honenuki, hoping for a miracle and too momentarily distracted to notice the hand that had brushed his shoulder.

Tetsutetsu's veins bulged and his face contorted in agony—defeat was close at hand. But just as Bakugo was about to claim victory, he rocked off-balance. It was the tatami mat under his feet.

"Huh?"

Tetsutetsu was too focused to recognize his opponent's shock for what it was, and his arm didn't miss a beat, pushing up and over with all its coiled energy and bringing Bakugo's hand down onto the table. Bakugo leaped away from the tatami mat that had nearly swallowed him up, furious that he'd been robbed of his victory.

"What the hell was that?" he shouted.

Midoriya glanced at the warped tatami mat and gasped.

"It's...been softened, by Honenuki's Quirk?"

"Softening," as the name implied, allowed Honenuki to soften any nonliving object with a single touch.

"It wasn't me! I didn't do it!" cried Honenuki, indignant at Midoriya's accusation. No other Quirk in the room was capable of such a thing, except...

"Damn you to hell!" shouted Bakugo toward Monoma, who had nearly made it out the door without being noticed.

"To hell? For what, exactly?" said Monoma, feigning ignorance. His Quirk was "Copy," which let him copy anyone else's Quirk for five minutes after touching them.

"We all know that was you, just now!"

"Hmm? What was me? You would dare to treat me like a criminal without any proof again?"

Another shrill laugh, and the boy was out the door.

"Sorry, I'd better get back there too! Good luck," said Kirishima, suddenly remembering his own lessons.

"I'll kill that copycat bastard!" shouted Bakugo.

"H-he's really not that bad once you get to know him..." said Shoda, feeling like another apology was in order. Kendo might have solved the Monoma problem with a swift chop to the neck, but for better or worse, the girls were in the middle of their slumber party.

"So... What happens now?" asked Ojiro, turning to Ida.

"Hrm... Shall we start over...?" said Ida.

"No freaking way! I was about to win there!" spat Bakugo.

"Nuh-uh! I made a solid comeback at the end!" countered Tetsutetsu. With their honorable match interrupted, the two were back to petty squabbling.

Ida grumbled, desperately trying to think of a solution that would satisfy all. Midoriya had the same thought, and his eureka moment came when his eyes settled on one corner of the room.

"Um, we could compete again, but this time with a pillow fight?" said Midoriya. In one corner of the boys' large room, their futons were stacked high with a pile of pillows on top.

"But, Midoriya, pillows were not made to be weapons," said Ida.

"True, but... Look, this could be a way to settle our argument where nobody actually gets hurt."

"I must agree that is a fantastic feature of your pillow proposal, but…"

Ida still seemed unconvinced, so the other boys chimed in, clearly excited about such a staple of overnight field trips.

"Pillow fight, let's do it!"

"My blood's already pumping just thinking about it!"

No need to tally the votes—referee Ida agreed to the pillow fight. Class A was at a numbers disadvantage, though, so class B had to draft a select team of eight members.

From A, Midoriya, Todoroki, Bakugo, Tokoyami, Shoji, Aoyama, Ojiro, and Koda.

From B, Tetsutetsu, Honenuki, Awase, Shoda, Shishida, Kosei Tsuburaba, Sen Kaibara, and Kojiro Bondo.

Ida would continue in his role as referee.

The boys weren't sure about the "official" rules for pillow fighting, so they came up with their own. A five-minute time limit, and five pillows in play, total. Like in dodgeball, catching a pillow meant one was safe. Getting hit and dropping the pillow meant one was out. Whichever team had more surviving mem-

bers at the end would win. No Quirk use allowed, of course. The line dividing the teams ran down the very center of the room, and the nonparticipating class B boys sat in one corner, cheering on their classmates.

"Get ready to cry this time, you goons," said Bakugo, issuing what was a pretty low-key threat, for him.

"Not a chance! Class B forever!" fired back Tetsutetsu.

"Pillow fight or not, treat these pillows with care!" said the referee. "As you throw them, spare a thought for the craftspeople who created these objects!"

Midoriya was fairly certain those craftspeople had never imagined this use for their pillows, but he held his tongue, since the game was about to begin.

UA

"Let the pillow fight commence!"

No sooner had Ida spoken than the pillows started flying, whizzing past each other with unreasonable speed and force, for pillows. Getting hit by one might actually hurt. But for the time being, there was only catching and counterthrows, with blinding pillow-based assaults from every angle and direction.

"Very impressive!" said Ida, struggling to remain focused enough to execute his duties. It was impressive, though—neither side was budging, and all players were still in the game after several minutes.

"To your right, Midoriya!"

"Thanks, Tokoyami!"

Tokoyami's quick warning helped Midoriya dodge one of Honenuki's throws, coming in at a dead angle. Right at the dividing line, Bakugo leaped and aimed a pillow square at Tetsutetsu.

"Naptime for you, metalhead!"

"Won't catch me sleeping on the job!"

As promised, Tetsutetsu caught Bakugo's killer toss at point-blank range and threw the pillow right back.

"Eat my Iron Beast Bomber!"

The brutal combos and bombastic back-and-forth went on, the casual game having long since surpassed the realm of an ordinary pillow fight. This was war.

"Incredible!" said Midoriya, starting in again. "Battling on a team like this is perfect for any number of simulations, and having five pillows in play means a

high frequency of attacks. So we have to defend while fighting back, striking a balance. Plus, we can come up with strategies to..."

Todoroki caught a pillow before it could nail the mumbling Midoriya.

"Think later, Midoriya. Act now."

"Oh, sorry, Todoroki!"

"Focus up, you damn nerd!" said Bakugo.

Before they knew it, the five minutes were up.

"We have a tie game!" announced Ida, unable to hide his glowing admiration for both teams of warriors. Not a single boy had been knocked out, but in a way that was only natural, since the practical exercises of the Hero Course had already honed their bodies in the few months since school had started. They'd grown too agile and adept to be taken down by a mere tossed pillow.

"What now?"

"We go again, duh!"

It was like they were back in elementary school, ready to explode with excitement at the drop of a hat. But the excitement soon waned, especially when the second round also ended in a tie. And the third, and the fourth.

"Ugh, just settle this already!" came a shout from the class B spectators, and the pillow fighters felt the same way. This draining tournament was already coming after a full day of Quirk training, which was now taking a toll on their energy levels. They wanted it to be over, but every round ended in a tie. A single thought passed through the exhausted boys' minds.

What if they could use their Quirks?

The fifth round began.

"Take this! My Iron Buster Cannon!"

Bakugo caught Tetsutetsu's throw, just as he had countless times. His frustration was building to the bursting point.

"Gotta say, you come up with the lamest attack names, dammit!"

"Huh? No way! My attacks are ultracool!"

"Yeah, if you think ancient fighting games are cool!"

"That's rich, coming from 'Lord Explosion Murder'!" quipped Tetsutetsu, referring to the code name Bakugo had come up with during class—a name rejected for being distinctly unheroic sounding.

"Gah! Lord Explosion Murder's better than your crap, metalhead!" screamed Bakugo. A small explosion

burst from his palm during his next throw, set off by the nitroglycerin-like sweat created by his Quirk. It wasn't on purpose—the earlier training had succeeded in enlarging his pores, making the explosions that much easier to trigger.

"Stop, stop! Bakugo, use of Quirks is a violation of the rules!" shouted Ida.

"Wasn't trying to! It just happened!"

Upon hearing Bakugo's excuse, a few of the wearier boys gasped. Accidental Quirk use would be overlooked?

"Resume!"

The first one to react to Ida's command was Tsuburaba, a listless class B boy with notably round eyes. He coughed exaggeratedly to disguise a quick exhale that created an invisible barrier in midair. Tsuburaba's Quirk was "Solid Air," which let him transform his breath into floating shields and platforms.

"Oops, my bad!"

"And accidents don't count, right?" said Awase, who wasted no time in using Tsuburaba's solid air as a foothold, leaping nearly to the ceiling to chuck a pillow at a dumbstruck Koda. But Ojiro threw himself in front of his classmate, using his prehensile tail to catch Awase's missile.

"Tsuburaba! Ojiro! Quirks are forbidden in this game!" chided Ida.

"Sorry! But they did it first," said Ojiro, looking distressed. Meanwhile, a wicked grin arose on Bakugo's face.

"Right, sure, accidents don't count... Fair enough... So my bad if this kills ya!" said Bakugo, tossing an explosion-powered pillow at Tsuburaba. The target didn't have time to create a new shield, but the pillow bounced off the existing solidified air overhead.

"My bad over here, too!" said Honenuki, who'd already touched a few of the tatami mats on the class A side of the battlefield, softening them. He, Awase, and Kaibara took the chance to pepper their opponents with pillows.

"Whoa!" yelped Midoriya, who used his Quirk to leap high into the air, dodging the pillows and escaping the softened floor simultaneously. "One For All" granted Midoriya prodigious power that had been stockpiled and passed down through the generations.

Nearby, Tokoyami's Dark Shadow lifted Aoyama out

of harm's way, while Todoroki's "Half-Cold Half-Hot" created ice platforms, allowing him to rescue Koda and Shoji. Bakugo was, of course, firing off explosions with every pillow he threw.

"I guess we're all allowed to use our Quirks now?" asked Todoroki, a bit bewildered.

"Erm, still against the rules, but we kinda don't have a choice...?" said Midoriya, at somewhat of a loss.

"What's the meaning of this? Stop using your Quirks at once!" screamed referee Ida from the sidelines, swinging his arms like mad and eliciting a series of "My bad!" and "That was an accident!" from the participants.

"Why're you guys breaking the rules, huh?" asked Tetsutetsu.

"This was supposed to be a fair battle!" added Shoda.

"But this was never going to end otherwise! Oops, my bad!" said Honenuki as he picked up a pillow. Shoji caught Honenuki's projectile with one of his dupli-arm tentacles and spoke from a mouth on a neighboring tentacle.

"If our opponents can't help all these 'accidents,' then neither can we."

With tentacles spread like wings, Shoji caught a number of pillows at once and threw them all back at full force.

"*My bad.*"

"It's only logical... Now go, Dark Shadow! But not on purpose!" said Tokoyami.

"Yep, my bad too!" added Dark Shadow, Tokoyami's birdlike familiar. The creature swooped across the battlefield, catching every last pillow thrown by class B and returning the favor.

Midoriya surveyed the scene and began muttering again.

"Of course, Shoji's Quirk makes him well suited to catching multiple objects at once! And throwing them back, even. Why, he could even deal with a mad bomber that way, assuming the bombs weren't overly powerful... Hmm. Oh, but Tokoyami's Dark Shadow could just carry the bombs a safe distance away! Tsuburaba's Quirk is also quite versatile. Those shields are invisible, and he doesn't make much noise while creating them. Perfect for an approach from above in a hostage situation... Wow, so many possibilities!"

MY HERO ACADEMIA SCHOOL BRIEFS

"Quit yer babbling, Deku!" roared Bakugo. He spun around and launched a pillow at Midoriya.

"I'm on *your* team, Kacchan!"

"Just shut up already! It's distracting!"

Dark Shadow playfully caught a pillow hurled by Shishida and said "More pillows, more fun!" before grabbing every last pillow from the reserve pile in the corner.

"Dark Shadow's having a bit too much fun, no?" said Todoroki.

"Enough, Dark Shadow! This is no game—our pride as men is at stake," said Tokoyami, scolding his familiar.

"I thought it was steak at stake? Or pork, non? ☆" said Aoyama, who was attempting to hide and take a breather. But a blob of white liquid from Bondo's Quirk, "Cemedine," made its mark and hardened Aoyama to the floor where he crouched.

"Will you all please listen! No more Quirks, I said!" shouted Ida in vain, just as Monoma returned for the third time.

"Well, this has certainly escalated," he said.

Class B was clearly struggling to defend against

Bakugo's explosion-powered pillows, while Shoji and Dark Shadow provided ironclad defense. Tsuburaba, Honenuki, and Bondo had their own defensive and disruptive tricks, but team B was lacking attacks with any real punch.

"Crud, we might actually lose this!" groaned Tetsutetsu.

Awase said "Oh, I know!" and ran around whispering his plan to everyone but Tetsutetsu and Shoda, all while dodging class A's attacks. Each class B boy nodded at Awase in turn and began passing him any and all pillows they caught. By the time class A noticed, Awase had amassed a mountain of pillows.

"Don't stop throwing, you!" said Bakugo.

"Cram it! This is a valid strategy!" shot back Awase.

"A strategy I'm wholeheartedly on board with!" said Monoma, who'd managed to sneak to the back of class B's territory without anyone noticing.

"You again, Monoma?"

The last thing class A expected was for the enemy strategists' eyes to flash red.

"Do it now!" shrieked Monoma.

"Creeping around again, copycat? Wait...huh?"

said Bakugo, shooting a glance down at his own hand in disbelief. No explosion issued forth. Sensing something was up, Midoriya tried to rush over with a burst of One For All, but that failed too.

"Is he...using Aizawa Sensei's Quirk?" gasped Midoriya.

Monoma grinned suggestively, his eyes bulging wide, unblinking.

"That's right. I plucked a bit of lint off your dear teacher's shoulder and managed to touch him in the process. So now's your chance, Awase!"

"G-got it!"

Awase had used his Quirk, "Weld," to fuse the pillows together on the atomic level, thereby forming one massive monster pillow. One far too large to catch. And since Monoma had copied Aizawa's "Erasure," Todoroki couldn't even throw up an ice wall to protect the boys of class A.

"Heave ho!"

The class B boys joined forces to lift the pillow, and even Tetsutetsu and Shoda—who'd been protesting the use of Quirks just a moment earlier—decided to cooperate at the last second.

"Dirty rotten cheaters!" shouted Bakugo.

"All's fair in love and war, I'm afraid! Throw it now, boys!" shouted Monoma.

They reared back, stepped forward, and sent the jumbo pillow flying just as the room's sliding screen snapped open.

"What do you think you're doing in h—"

"Argh!"

The ultra pillow had flown far. As far as the doorway, in fact, where it smacked into the homeroom teachers of classes A and B, Aizawa and Vlad King. The two had grown suspicious of the ruckus coming from the boys' room as well as Monoma's oddly frequent bathroom breaks.

Every last boy went pale.

"You wanna explain yourselves?" shouted the imposingly muscular Vlad King, whose roar froze the class B boys in place. "This is an embarrassment! Using your Quirks for a silly game...? Have you forgotten why you're here? To train for your provisional licenses, you little fools!"

"W-we're sorry, Sensei!"

They were practically in tears.

"We said this time was your own, but that didn't entitle you to this sort of idiocy... Still, very good to know you've all got so much energy to burn."

Aizawa, meanwhile, remained silent, but his icy stare was enough to send chills down his students' spines. He didn't need to speak a word to communicate his rage, and the boys of class A were too terrified even to attempt a meek apology.

The homeroom teachers were like substitute parents to these kids, and in the teachers' minds, the students might as well have been their own children. Each man had his own methods and theories on education, but both agreed that it was their duty to punish trouble-makers as necessary.

"Energy to burn, yes... Why don't we double tomorrow's training for this bunch, Vlad?" said Aizawa, finally speaking up.

"Great idea!" said Vlad.

"B-but!"

Today's training had been harsh enough, so the boys couldn't help but balk at the suggestion. A piercing glare from Aizawa quickly silenced them.

"Still have the energy to protest, even? Three times the training, then."

The boys choked back their outcry with tears in their eyes. Any more training might actually kill them. Aizawa's lesson still wasn't over, though.

"This all started over the matter of tomorrow's dinner, right? So it's only appropriate...that you boys go without any meat at all!" said Aizawa.

"Nooo!"

"Forcing us to go vegetarian? Too cruel!"

"Want to lose the potatoes too?" suggested Aizawa.

And so, the teachers brought an end to the fateful clash between classes A and B, handing both a stunning loss of sorts. The boys would no doubt find themselves fighting fiercely for things that mattered someday, whether that be pride, meat, or something bigger. But while that burning passion could do a lot of good, the would-be heroes had to be careful not to stray from the path. That's where lessons like this one came into play. Lessons to keep them on the road to becoming true heroes.

Part 6
After the Hubbub

A sudden pop, and Tenya Ida's eyes snapped open. It was his own bursting snot bubble that had done it, but Ida was still emerging from dreamland and was barely aware. Surrounded by complete darkness, he had to blink a few times to confirm he was actually awake. A nearby snore sealed the deal, reminding Ida where he was, and why. He wasn't one to suffer a sloppy sleep cycle—he took pride in his regulated lifestyle, choosing specific bedtimes and deciding precisely when to awaken. After all, that sort of discipline was the first step toward a mature, independent adulthood. In the dark, Ida grimaced at this particular failing, as lack of proper sleep would mean less stamina the following day, and this training camp demanded stamina above all else.

I ought to get right back to sleep, then.

But that certain someone kept snoring, and the sound had penetrated Ida's consciousness. He couldn't not hear it anymore. Still, the snorer wasn't acting intentionally, so Ida couldn't hold it against him. Whoever he was, he must be just as tired as Ida was.

We did endure quite a day, today.

Though it had technically been yesterday, it was close enough in memory that Ida still thought of it as "today." Starting at 5:30 a.m., the students of classes A and B had trained to strengthen their Quirks. Then they'd made curry for dinner, which wasn't as good as the sort served in restaurants but was still a welcome relief for their empty bellies. Most had taken seconds. After dinner, they had had the squabble with class B over nikujaga meat and, finally, a good scolding from Aizawa.

If only I had been a better leader!

In the dark silence, Ida blamed himself for failing in his capacity as referee.

Aizawa had also laid into Minoru Mineta for his peeping attempt, so the combined lecture had gone on until bedtime, just about. Wary that Mineta might

try creeping into the girls' room during the night, the boys had wrapped their smallest classmate in his own futon, like a sushi roll. He'd begged them to use ropes instead—it was anyone's guess why—but nobody was in the mood to honor the request.

The snoring stopped, almost too suddenly. Ida gasped.

What if this individual suffers from sleep apnea...?

Fearing for his classmate's life, Ida leaped up and, on instinct, reached for his glasses next to his pillow. His hand struck empty, though—his glasses case simply wasn't there. His vision was a respectable 20/25 even without glasses, but Ida never wanted to miss a thing, so he opted to use the corrective lenses at all times. In this case, he kept calm and pressed on without them, as the snorer's well-being came first. Based on the direction and intensity, it had to have been Rikido Sato.

"Hey. Sato..."

"Zzz... Zzz... Too much. So full..."

Ida was relieved to know that Sato's irregular breathing had been a temporary anomaly.

Thank heavens... Goodness, though—he's been tossing and turning.

Sato had kicked his bedding off, leaving him exposed to the still air of the room, so Ida gently replaced the blanket atop his classmate. Summer or not, the chill of night could still do a lot of harm.

"Hmm?"

The room wasn't pitch-dark, per se, and as Ida's eyes adjusted, the faint light penetrating the room's shoji doors from outside revealed that more of his classmates were not exactly sound sleepers. Plenty had arms and legs dangling off their futons, or worse. Ida couldn't imagine taking such a slovenly approach to slumber.

"It's as if they're just begging to catch colds," whispered Ida to himself as he set out to right these wrongs, since he would've had a hard time falling back asleep knowing his friends might suffer. He also needed a trip to the bathroom. That made two tasks on the agenda before Ida could curl back up into his own futon. Well, three.

First, my glasses…

Ida might as well have been missing a limb. He searched again, but the case was nowhere near his pillow, nor buried under his futon.

Where could they have gotten to…? Ah, perhaps…

Maybe one of his thrashing classmates had accidentally kicked his glasses case across the room?

I might as well continue my search while tucking them all back in, then...

Ever the Boy Scout, Ida had brought several backup pairs of glasses on this trip—concerned that some might be chewed up and spit out by the harsh training—but to misplace a pair outright would be to disrespect the craftsperson who made them.

Here I go...

Koji Koda was closest to Sato and had half of his body exposed to the indoor elements, so Ida began by fixing the quiet, animal-loving boy's bedding. He also swept the area around Koda and Sato, since odds were the glasses case was nearby. No such luck, though.

He moved on to Izuku Midoriya, who slept closest to Ida's own futon. Midoriya lay on his side and issued regular, gentle breaths, but his blanket covered only his lower half. When Ida tugged it up to his shoulder, Midoriya mumbled and squirmed a bit but showed no sign of waking. He must've been having a pleasant dream, since he chuckled like a kid with candy. Ida himself couldn't help but smile at this, and it reassured him that this mission to ensure restful sleep for his friends was a worthy one. More rigorous training awaited them all in just a few hours, so the class president was determined to see his electorate well rested and prepared.

Riding this momentum, Ida carefully searched around Midoriya's futon for the glasses, but still nothing. He moved toward Midoriya's neighbor, Shoto Todoroki, and was shocked to find that the boy had somehow flipped around completely, with his feet on his pillow where his head ought to have been.

I would expect Todoroki to sleep more soundly than this...

Ida was conflicted. Should he try to realign his friend, placing head on pillow? No, that was likely to wake him up, so all Ida did was replace Todoroki's blanket.

"Hrmm..."

A pained grumble. A concerned Ida drew close enough to see Todoroki's face contort and his forehead shimmer with a cold sweat, suggesting that he was in the throes of a nightmare. Perhaps waking him would be the right thing to do, if he were actually unwell?

Todoroki's mouth puckered bitterly, and he started sleep talking.

"Hope you choke on that *kuzumochi*..."

Kuzumochi? Why?

Ida couldn't have known that Endeavor, Todoroki's father, was partial to kuzumochi.

If he's merely dreaming of food, perhaps it's best to let sleeping dogs lie...?

The search for the glasses case continued to no avail, so Ida moved on to the next troubled sleeper. He spied a boy facedown, propped up on his knees, head buried in a pile of pillows.

I commend whomever this is for successfully falling asleep in that position...

Ida carefully removed the pillows one at a time and quickly recognized the bright shock of hair underneath.

Oh. It's Kaminari.

After Ida had gone to bed, Denki Kaminari and the rest of the remedial crowd had returned from their lessons and enjoyed their own little pillow fight in silence, which had resulted in the spectacle Ida now stumbled across. How Kaminari had managed to fall

asleep like that was a mystery, but the class president decided only to replace the blanket and continued the search for his glasses.

While groping between the futons, Ida nearly missed the arm that came thrusting at him from behind.

"Hiyahh!"

Ida spun around just in time to glimpse a sharpened, bladelike hand and dodge out of the way. Eijiro Kirishima had activated his Hardening Quirk in his sleep, and his knife hand pierced straight through a stray pillow. Ida's tuck and roll landed him next to another messy sleeper—Katsuki Bakugo.

"Escaped by a hair..." remarked Ida to himself.

Kirishima exhaled in short puffs while continuing to stab at Kaminari's pillows, as if in the middle of a training exercise. Ida sighed and replaced Kirishima's blanket. They'd all slept like logs the previous night— their first at the lodge—so it hadn't occurred to Ida how much trouble their Quirks might cause while bunking together.

Bakugo's midriff was fully exposed, so Ida was sure to fix his blanket as well. Then Sero's, though Sero himself had rolled off his futon straight onto the floor, near Bakugo's feet. Something soft fwumped against Ida—it was Bakugo's blanket, replaced only moments ago. The boy must've been feeling overheated.

We can't have your abdomen getting cold, though, Bakugo.

Ida pulled the blanket just up to Bakugo's chest, but the kick that shoved it off this time seemed to scream, "Don't test me!" Bakugo was Bakugo, even in his sleep. Ida tried again several times, until his classmate was apparently perturbed enough to fire off a small explosion from one palm.

"Ack!"

Ida instinctively turned away from the bright flash, and in that instant, he spotted what looked like his glasses case a few feet away, between Mashirao Ojiro and Mezo Shoji. He gave up on Bakugo's blanket, opting instead to tug the boy's tank top down over his stomach, ever so gingerly.

Let's check over here…

But in racing to his glasses, Ida forgot to watch his step. He stomped down hard on Ojiro's tail, which was drooping off the futon to one side, and it took Ida a

second to realize what had been squished underfoot.

The tail was like a third arm to Ojiro. For many animals, the versatile tail could express emotions, warn allies of danger, and so on, so it was only natural that Ojiro reacted violently to Ida's unwitting assault. Though Ojiro himself remained asleep, the tail awoke, grabbed the offender, and flung him into the air.

Ida landed squarely in Shoji's arms, which quickly bound him in a full choke hold. Shoji must've been battling a villain in his dream, because he squeezed Ida with a brute strength that none in the class could match. Ida's life flashed before his eyes, but more dire was the sudden pressure on his already stressed bladder. He attempted to tap out, as if to cry uncle, but Shoji had no intention of releasing whatever villain had invaded his dreams.

What saved Ida turned out to be Kaminari, who happened to roll toward Shoji's futon with a "Yayyy..." In his desperate struggle, Ida lashed out and grabbed ahold of one of Kaminari's ankles.

"Nngyah?"

Kaminari's eyes popped open for a second as he discharged a burst of electricity. Shoji flinched at the loud zap and flash of light, giving Ida a brief window to escape his grip and roll away.

Another "Yayyy…" from Kaminari, who fell back asleep instantly. Ida breathed a sigh of relief but quickly realized he'd lost track of his glasses again.

Where could they be now…?

Ida moved toward Yuga Aoyama, at one end of the mass of futons. The boy's blanket was displaced, revealing his dramatic pose as he slept, like something out of a Renaissance fresco. Ida covered up Aoyama and scanned the area, but still no glasses. Nearby, Fumikage Tokoyami lay faceup and perfectly still, wrapped impeccably in his blanket. The boy's shallow breathing was the only indicator that he really was sleeping.

Tokoyami is the image of discipline, even in his sleep!

Ida gave an approving nod and moved on to Mineta, still bundled in his futon like a pig in a blanket. No chance that he'd be afflicted by night chills, at least.

"Bring 'em on… Keep the boobs coming!" mumbled Mineta, causing Ida to wonder what sort of dream the boy might possibly be having. But the class president suddenly realized that something was off about Mineta's

silhouette. In addition to the perfectly round pop-off balls on his head, there was a smaller oval shape.

"Hmm? I've found them!"

Ida clamped his hands over his own mouth, having spoken louder than he meant to. After confirming that everyone was still sound asleep, he approached Mineta's literal bedroll. The oval was the glasses case, of course, stuck fast to one of Mineta's head balls.

This does present a problem...

Ida's joy faded instantly, and he crossed his arms in thought. Anything stuck to Mineta's balls couldn't be ripped away for a full day, so even if the glasses case had gotten stuck around bedtime, it would be many hours, at least, before it would fall off of its own accord. Mineta himself could have torn the ball in question from his own head, but Ida wasn't about to awaken his classmate. He was entitled to his sleep and dreams, if nothing else.

I'll just have to extract my glasses, then.

Ida turned to face Mineta's head and crouched, planning to open the case ever so carefully and remove the glasses. Fortunately, only half of the case adhered to the ball's surface, leaving the hinge free to swivel.

Ida's fingers slowly moved toward their target, but Mineta started squirming.

"I toldja to bring me every last boob in this shop..."

Ida was perplexed. Breasts normally came attached to bodies, so how could a salesperson bring them out to a customer in discrete units? The notion of such a Boobatorium was patently absurd, even for a dream. The line of thought gave Ida pause and stayed his hand.

What if his fingers got stuck? Mineta would awaken without a doubt, and even if he agreed to pluck the offending ball from his head, Ida would still be left with a handful of sticky ball for the next half a day or more. Going to the bathroom and feeding himself, even, would become nearly impossible chores.

Ida hesitated and wondered if he should take care of his bladder first. No—all he had to do was get the case open. Simple. He composed himself, breathed deeply, and reached toward the stuck case once again with all the caution and precision of a professional bomb diffuser. His trembling fingers were nearly there.

"I said, bring out every last jiggly one you've got! The boobs of this world are my rightful property!"

The bizarre outburst made Ida flinch and retreat in

spite of himself, and Mineta's burrito bedding started to roll.

"No, wait, don't run from me, boobs!" cried Mineta, apparently in hot pursuit of his desires within the dream.

"G-get back here!" whispered Ida, pursuing the pursuer. Mineta's bed bundle deftly dodged between two of his classmate's futons but was on a collision course with Kirishima. Bound tightly or not, there was no stopping Mineta when he was after this particular quarry.

"Watch out… Ah!"

Mineta crashed into Kirishima, and the impact sprung open the case, sending the glasses flying. Even in the dark, Ida tracked the arc they traced overhead, glinting like a shooting star in the night sky. A flash of despair—a fall from that height could break the glasses, or worse, injure a classmate, depending on where the hapless victim was struck. Already leaping into action, Ida prayed they'd land atop a soft futon. He couldn't in good conscience activate his noisy "Engine" Quirk, so he watched helplessly as the glasses fell toward Tokoyami.

"Tokoyami, watch ou—"

Then, a miracle that made Ida gasp. Tokoyami's arms swung open midflight like a pair of wings, and the glasses spun about before landing squarely on top of Tokoyami's beaked face, as neatly as if he'd decided to try them on himself. Yet he remained fast asleep.

Ida had to catch himself. It is the sheer rarity of a miracle that defines a miracle, and Ida had a desperate urge to share with someone what he'd just witnessed. But to awaken a classmate at this point would be to spit in the face of the minor miracle of the glasses and all of Ida's efforts thus far, so he sighed, plucked the glasses from Tokoyami's face, and finally set out for the bathroom. Before closing the sliding screen to the room, the class president surveyed his soundly sleeping classmates one last time.

UA

Having finished his business, an unusually refreshed Ida was heading back to the room when an odd clicking noise made him stop. He followed the sound down the

dim corridor and found the door to the lodge's office. A bit of light seeped through the gap around the frame.

"This year's crop of first-years seem like fun kids, though."

It was Mandalay's voice. The clicking and clacking continued.

Ida was still puzzled, but more than that, he felt a wave of appreciation that one of his hosts was still hard at work this late. Before he could turn away, though, he heard another voice.

"Very sorry for the trouble earlier."

Ah. It's Aizawa Sensei.

His homeroom teacher's unaffected drawl froze Ida in place. The competition between the boys and Mineta's peeping attempt, in particular, were disturbances that Aizawa now felt the need to apologize for.

If only I had performed my duties as class president!

Ida pursed his lips and silently cursed his own negligence. He should've kept a closer eye on Mineta. He should've brought the matter of the nikujaga meat to a less chaotic resolution.

Sensei shouldn't have to bear this burden alone. I should be in there too, apologizing...

Now Pixie-Bob's jaunty voice rang out, as if to make light of Ida's grim determination.

"Relaaax, it's fine. We get it. High schoolers are bound to go a little *wild* now and then."

"Still, though…"

The next voice, also wracked with guilt, was Vlad King's.

"Our kids went a little too wild, this time. They can't afford these sorts of distractions leading up to their licensing exam. Besides, the test of courage tomorrow was supposed to be the time for them to cut loose."

"I wouldn't sweat it," replied Pixie-Bob. "High school's the time when kids are desperate to have some fun. And your Hero Course cuties are stuck following the straight and narrow every darn day, right?"

"Those who think like that could never cut it in the Hero Course," said Aizawa.

Ida took in a sharp breath. Aizawa's tone was sharp as ever, but his words revealed the deep trust he had in his students.

He still has so much faith in us, despite our earlier failings…

U.A. High was not a school for the faint of heart. It set up mercilessly high hurdles and commanded its students to surpass them. But Ida knew that this severity was compassion in disguise, as the institution and its educators, Aizawa among them, believed wholeheartedly that the students could meet these challenges. Yes, the future heroes had mentors who believed in their potential, and nothing could be more reassuring. With renewed gusto, Ida took a deep breath and puffed out his chest.

We must prove that that faith in us is justified and then surpass their expectations. In other words...

Plus Ultra.

With his school's motto resonating in his mind, Ida turned to leave. The priority here was certainly not bursting into the office and apologizing alongside his teacher. No, he would prove his worth during the next training session, which meant getting proper rest in the meantime.

What on earth was that clicking sound, though...?

Aizawa's faith in his students sent Ida back to the room in high spirits, so his question remained unanswered, and he never heard the rest of the conversation.

"And if slackers like that did come to us, they'd be expelled in no time. There... Two hidden *dora* tiles give me an eight-thousand-point win."

With that, Aizawa knocked over his winning set of mahjong tiles, shocking Vlad King, Mandalay, and Pixie-Bob.

"Two hidden dora?" roared Vlad.

Yes, it was a friendly game of mahjong that drew the teachers to the office this late at night. The game was to them what the pillow fight was to field tripping boys. Mahjong typically conjured an image of smoke-filled gambling halls, so perhaps it was for the best that the straitlaced Ida hadn't witnessed the entire scene. With this last round finally over, the spectating Ragdoll and Tiger stood up with satisfied looks on their faces.

"Should we call it a night? Got another early morning tomorrow," said Mandalay.

"Sounds good," said a weary Vlad King, nodding.

"One more game! Pleeease!" begged Pixie-Bob.

"How many has it been, already?" said Aizawa, glaring and fed up.

Pixie-Bob had a reason for wanting to play on—she was unhappily single, and the others had promised to introduce her to some decent men if she won a round of mahjong. Sadly, the most enthusiastic player had already lost twice to the least motivated one—Aizawa. More than shogi or go, mahjong was a game that relied on luck, so a win for Pixie-Bob would've seemed to her like a divine prophecy that her days of singlehood would soon be over.

"See you tomorrow, then... Or, I guess it's already today?" said Aizawa.

"Gonna be another intense day with you cool cats! Night!" added Vlad.

Mandalay waved good night to the two U.A. teachers as they left for their own sleeping quarters, while Ragdoll and Tiger kept teasing a supremely disappointed Pixie-Bob.

UA

"You've got a real knack for mahjong, Eraser," said Vlad.

"I'm about average," replied Aizawa, relieved to be free from the exhausting table game. He glanced out the hallway window at the velvety-black, star-filled sky—a reminder of how far they were from the lights and action of the big city.

"Those little imps, though..." snorted Vlad, whose mind had drifted back to the boys' unruly pillow fight.

"All the more reason to show them no mercy in a few hours."

"Ah... One thing, Eraser."

"Hmm?"

"You do realize my boys would've won that thing if we hadn't interrupted?"

Vlad King dropped the comment casually, but Aizawa swiveled toward him with a glare. Vlad could act nonchalant at times, but the hot-blooded man in fact felt a great deal of warmth for his students, as most homeroom teachers would. In matters of A versus B, he was bound to root for his own team.

"Yeah. I wonder," was the retort from an exhausted, annoyed Aizawa. He let the comment slide, but not because he felt any less fatherly toward his own kids. This prompted Vlad to shoot Aizawa a devilish grin

that the latter ignored, attempting to change the subject.

"Anyhow, they'll have to test for their provisional licenses soon."

"For sure. Speaking of, I hear the Hero Killer is mostly recovered?"

"That's what they say," said Aizawa.

The idealistic Hero Killer went by the moniker "Stain." The villain saw All Might as the only true hero out there and had attempted to purge society of what he saw as lesser, degenerate heroes by going on a mass-murdering spree. Ida's older brother, Tensei, was one victim who had barely survived his encounter with the Hero Killer. Ida had sought revenge against Stain and gotten help in the nick of time from Midoriya and Todoroki. The three boys had triumphed in battle, leaving Stain heavily injured and locked behind bars for the time being.

Though Stain's reign of terror had ended, his actions fed the imaginations of other such agents of evil—ones eking out existences in the shadows, kept down by modern society. The League of Villains, in particular, was all too eager to ride Stain's coattails and take advantage of these shifting tides. Aizawa knew the emboldened league might lash out at his students again, so when that time came, he wanted the hero hopefuls to have legal permission to defend themselves.

"Let's hope that's the last we hear of him, anyway," added Aizawa.

The wind rattled the windows.

Just a passing gust, but somehow ominous enough to fill Aizawa's heart with an unknowable dread. He furrowed his brow instinctively and glanced out the window again, still finding only darkness and stars.

Stars that knew of the malice drawing near.

A Note from the Creator

Chock full of everyday scenes from these characters'
lives that didn't make it into the manga! Fun!
I'd love to draw them at some point!

KOHEI HORIKOSHI

A Note from the Author

I always get kind of emotional and excited while reading the manga, but volume 11 really blew me away. When the crowd in the streets joined as one to cheer on All Might, I gave in and let the tears flow. All Might is just so amazing. Incidentally, this book is a glimpse behind the scenes of the training camp in the woods, so All Might doesn't make an appearance... I'm sorry about that. The ever-chatty class A takes center stage, and class B shows up too. Sit back and enjoy!

ANRI YOSHI

MY HERO ACADEMIA:
SCHOOL BRIEFS—TRAINING CAMP

Written by Anri Yoshi
Original story by Kohei Horikoshi
Cover and interior design by Shawn Carrico
Translation by Caleb Cook

BOKU NO HERO ACADEMIA YUUEI HAKUSHO © 2016 by Kohei Horikoshi, Anri Yoshi
All rights reserved.
First published in Japan in 2016 by SHUEISHA Inc., Tokyo.
English translation rights arranged by SHUEISHA Inc.

Published by VIZ Media, LLC
P.O. Box 77010
San Francisco, CA 94107

Library of Congress Cataloging-in-Publication Data

Names: Horikoshi, Kôohei, 1986- author, artist. | Yoshi, Anri, contributor. |
  Cook, Caleb D., translator.
Title: School briefs / Kohei Horikoshi, Anri Yoshi ; translation by Caleb
  Cook.
Description: San Francisco, CA : VIZ Media LLC, [2019] | Series: My hero
  academia: school briefs ; 2 | Summary: Midoriya, Ida, and the rest of
  Class A at U.A. High School attend a training camp in the woods, and
  although they are there to improve their superpowers, it is also an
  opportunity for them to have fun.
Identifiers: LCCN 2019005776 | ISBN 9781421582719 (paperback)
Subjects: | CYAC: Heroes--Fiction. | High school--Fiction. |
  Schools--Fiction. | Ability--Fiction. | Fantasy. | BISAC: FICTION / Media
  Tie-In.
Classification: LCC PZ7.1.H6636 Sc 2019 | DDC [Fic]--dc23
LC record available at https://lccn.loc.gov/2019005776

Printed in the U.S.A.

10 9 8 7 6 5 4 3 2 1
First printing, July 2019

viz.com

shonenjump.com